The Lake Mystery

NANCY E. CROFTS

Fulton Books, Inc.
Meadville, PA

Published by Fulton Books 2021

ISBN 978-1-63860-110-4 (paperback)
ISBN 978-1-63860-111-1 (digital)

Printed in the United States of America

In memory of "Smitty" (Mitchell Smith) and "Mitch" (Robert Mitchell), who were fostered by my family and me for over thirty years.

Additionally, to Donald Demicco, Joseph Gadacy, and the many others who lived with us and added so much to our lives. Along, of course, with my wonderful husband, Mark; son Billy; son Elliott; his wife, Clarice; Louie, our precious current foster-care individual; and everyone who encouraged me to share these characters with you.

Contents

To the Lake

"Hey, ladies, are you two about finished packing for the lake?" their father's voice drifted up the stairs to where the twins were busy bouncing on their suitcases, trying desperately to get the overstuffed luggage closed and latched.

"Carol will be here in the next five minutes, my beautiful daughters. We must be punctual."

Cresselley looked over at struggling Robin and giggled. That was the courtroom lawyer coming out in their father. What made this attention to promptness so amusing to his offspring was the indisputable fact that their sitter/companion had never once been on time in the two years she had worked off and on for their parent.

"Yes, Dad," the girls called down in unison, "we'll be right there."

"You know, you'll be back here at the house at least once a week to do laundry. You needn't pack as though you're going to Morocco for the summer."

"We know, Dad." The twins appeared at the top of the stairs, each dragging a suitcase and sporting a backpack. "Can't you stay with us in Grammy's cottage, just for a few days?" the girls pleaded. "We barely get to see you at all anymore."

Robert Spenser frowned. He knew his lengthy absences from the new home he had moved them into at the end of December was a great source of sadness for his girls, even as they appeared to be recovering from the sudden loss of their mother two years prior, better than he himself was managing.

"I know, girls, but I must finish this last big case for the firm. Then I promise, you'll get so sick of having me home, you'll call an Uber to get me on the next train back to New York."

The girls glanced at each other with a mutual look. "Sick of Dad? Not possible."

Mixed with skepticism that he would actually give up the New York law firm he had shaped and be content as a small-town lawyer in the community he had gladly departed as a young man. The best part about the move, without a doubt, was the presence of their attentive, loving grandmother who rarely left the sleepy, little, eastern Connecticut town.

"Carol bought a Prius?" Robin was genuinely surprised as the little, black hybrid pulled into the driveway and the pretty twenty-year-old brunette stepped out of the car. "Her new boyfriend must be an environmentalist."

"Or a car salesman," Cresselley speculated.

Their father chuckled and reminded his daughters that Carol did have an intelligent, responsible head on her shoulders. Robert Spenser knew Carol's father from high school and admired his early entrepreneurial spirit. Right after graduation, as a young man, he went to work for a local marina, which he eventually bought from the aging owner. That's how two years ago—when Robert picked up new kayak paddles at the boatyard and enjoyed a conversation with her father about their high school days—Carol had been hired to care for his precious daughters when they spent time at the lake.

"Okay, girls, pack it up." Carol grinned as she approached the trio.

Exiting the house through the front door, Robert extended his hand, and Carol shook it, glancing down momentarily at the three one-hundred-dollar bills he had deposited in her palm.

"For extras." He winked and turned to give his daughters one last group hug.

"Bye, Dad. We know the reception at the cottage is dismal, and there isn't any Wi-Fi, but we'll text you from the end of the dock and e-mail from the library."

"And don't forget, you promised to take us exploring that mysterious place you called the Crossroads," Robin added the reminder to their goodbyes.

It was heart-wrenching for the girls to watch their father standing alone on the lawn as they pulled away, but he had yet to sort out life after their mother, and both knew they would have to be patient.

As the little hybrid climbed the last long hill before the descent to the lake, Robin looked over at her twin with a divulging look. Both girls wondered if Carol would remember the family tradition they had eagerly introduced her to when she first came to stay with them in the summer two years ago.

As a tall, metal structure came into view, the twins sang out in unison, "When can we go up the fire tower?"

Whether Carol remembered or not, she played along. Pretending to drive right by, she suddenly swerved into the dirt space at the foot of the enormous lookout.

"How about now?" she suggested.

Her charges giggled. "Carol, you wouldn't set foot on the first rung."

"You're undeniably right, I wouldn't, and your father would fire me if I even considered letting you go up those nine flights by yourselves. Admit it, you both thought I'd forgotten about your little ritual, didn't you?"

"Carol, you're a good sport, and we love you for it." Cresselley smiled.

"Well, you better," their companion threatened lightheartedly as she backed away from the tower and headed down the hill toward the lake and their grandmother's beloved cottage.

Carol brought twice the luggage as the twins combined, but that was expected. The girls were keenly aware that she wasn't much for "roughing it" and always considered herself a diva, regardless of the climate or the living conditions. Fortunately for all, she had the downstairs bedroom, just off the kitchen, while the girls each had a room upstairs.

"Hey, Robbie," Cresselley taunted, "want the bigger bedroom this summer? I'm willing to switch if you want."

"Oh, no, you're not getting my view of the lake. You don't want to switch. You're afraid I might want the bigger bed."

Robin was right about her sister's motive, Cresselley loved the bigger bedroom. It had been their grandmother's when their father was young. And to Cresselley's delight, the room still had her touch—pretty wallpaper, a ruffled bedspread, an antique dresser with mirror, and a framed picture their father had made in sheet metal shop class when he was in high school. There were still the two single beds in Robin's room the girls had shared until two summers ago, and despite Robin's claims, the view of the lake was spectacular from both vantage points.

Cresselley peeked around the corner into Robin's room. "I don't feel like unpacking. Want to go drag out the kayaks?"

"Sure, I suppose you want to paddle around the point to see if that guy you thought was so cute last summer is there with his family again," Robin teased. Her twin protested, despite a deep blush.

The kayaks were stored under the cottage for protection during the snow-swept winter. The girls grabbed the paddles off the back porch and called out their intentions through Carol's open window.

"Okay, you two, but wear your life jackets."

"Always," they responded with a hint of bother.

The girls had been participating in a long list of water sports since a very young age. Their parents made certain both girls were well trained and respectful of the elements.

Robin loyally crawled under the porch and tugged on the bow of her red boat. "Here, Elly, I'll slide it out and toss you the line so you can pull it free while I go back under for yours. I know you're a baby about spiders."

The manner in which the cottage was constructed more than a half a century ago was also a factor. It was built into the side of the hill with the front porch sitting on pylons made of large cement blocks. There was ample storage in that section facing the water, but it gradually became a tight crawlspace as the hill sloped upward underneath, and the back of the structure was practically resting on the ground. The family rumor circulating for three generations maintained that the unique bungalow was the brainchild of a local plumber who had assembled his friends, vague acquaintances, and a keg of beer one weekend. Allegedly, the little group of dubious artisans had "tossed up" the entire composition in a mere two days. Grammy never actually affirmed or denied the story, but the curtain rods and all the banisters were made from pipes, which did lend a certain amount of credibility to the legend. Apparently, the plumber had some financial tribulations a few years later, and Gram jumped at the chance to purchase waterfront property three miles from the family's residence. The girls' father had a plethora of wonderful summer memories lakeside, much like his daughters were in the process of compiling.

"What do you think, El? Should we pull out Dad's kayak too?" Robin emerged from under the cottage, draped in cobwebs. "What are you laughing at?" she demanded, running one hand through her hair and stifling a sneeze with the other.

"Not laughing," Cresselley denied.

"You didn't answer my question, Dad's kayak, maybe the canoe instead? Who knows? Carol might surprise us and jump on board one day in the next two months."

Cresselley looked doubtful but agreed with the idea of the canoe. "I think if Carol decided to become waterborne, she'd be more comfortable with someone else at the helm, so to speak."

"Good point, and Dad?"

Neither twin dared predict their father's behavior for the summer.

"Well," Robin offered, "he can always crawl under here, or one of us can join him in the canoe."

Cresselley was silent, but she nodded in agreement.

"Okay then, I'm done. Let's put on our life jackets and hit the open water!"

The lake sparkled brilliantly in the diamond sunlight as the girls paddled their way past Gram's dock and around the point. There was no sign of the teenage boy close to their age or his family that Cresselley secretly hoped to spot. The cottage they had rented the previous summer remained closed for the winter. Robin could sense her twin's disappointment and bigheartedly did not tease her. The girls paddled silently by the empty summer home and continued in the warm sun, with Robin lagging behind. As the opposite shoreline came into view, Cresselley stopped abruptly. She looked behind her to see an inattentive Robin leaning back, at ease in her drifting kayak, soaking up the sun.

"Robbie, catch up!" she called out behind her.

"Why are we suddenly in a hurry?"

"Stop messing around and get over here. You need to see what I'm seeing."

Robin sat up at the sound of urgency in her sister's tone and began paddling vigorously. She hadn't quite caught up when Cresselley's words took her off guard.

"We never heard that the Barkers' house burned down." Cresselley was adamant. "They've owned that property almost as long as Grammy's had hers."

Startled, Robin followed her sister's gaze to the charred house ruins, which had been one of the few year-round occupancies zoned legally on the lake.

"I wonder why Grammy didn't tell us. She must have known."

"Man, I don't know, but it would have rattled the whole lake community. I hope the Barkers are all right, I wonder where they are now."

The girls resumed paddling side by side, headed for a closer look at the site of the fire. As they closed in on the Barkers' beach, it was obvious that the tragedy had occurred recently, probably not more than three months ago. What really got their attention though was the yellow caution tape, POLICE LINE. DO NOT CROSS, often used to cordon off a crime scene.

"How did we miss this?" Cresselley questioned with astonishment. "This must have happened after we moved into the new house last December. I don't remember hearing about it or seeing it anywhere on social media."

"I have no idea, but I wouldn't be surprised if it has something to do with the police presence, and of course, you can only notice the remains from the water. You never were able to spot the house from the road. I suppose if the authorities wanted to hush it up, it wouldn't be that difficult."

The girls leaned on their paddles and drifted slowly with the light breeze, dumbfounded.

"Should we ask someone what happened, or pretend we didn't notice?" Cresselley wondered.

"I think when we see Gram next, we should casually ask how the Barkers are." Robin looked thoughtful. "You know, El, she really might not know. Think about it. How would something like this have escaped the whole town unless some powerful agency had prohibited the release of any information?"

"You're right. And Gram never would have seen it in person. It's in the southwest cove. The only people who might have noticed were the next-door neighbors, and they haven't even opened their place up for the season yet."

"Let's paddle on, El." Robin turned the bow of her kayak. "This is starting to creep me out."

"How about visiting another part of the lake? Want to go around Gilligan's Island? Better yet, a trip down the Amazon, that's always thrilling."

"You hate the Amazon!" Robin declared. "There's always a bunch of turtles, snakes, and fallen trees that look like alligators in there."

"I know, I was trying to impress you and forget about the Barkers."

"Are you up for the boat launch?" Robin suggested. "It's pretty neutral."

The girls headed off to the west side of the lake with synchronized strokes. It was a decent workout to the other side, past the four islands, two of which the "Amazon" cut through. They were still a distance away when the girls stopped abruptly. There was a line of orange cones blocking the entrance to the state access.

"Okay, now I *really* wish Dad had stayed. Why on earth would the launch be closed?" Cresselley glanced over at her sister with a look that read anxiety.

The girls hadn't noticed, until this latest detection, how uncannily quiet the lake was for such a beautiful afternoon. But now, the absence of outboard boats pulling kneeboarders and tubers was starkly apparent. Without the state ramp access, visitors and even some residents would have no means to put their crafts in the water.

"Let's get back, Robbie, this is too creepy."

The girls headed back to shore without further speculation.

Carol looked up from where she was reading the morning paper on the dock and noticed their unusual demeanor. "The two of you look like you encountered pirates or maybe a great white shark."

"We wish," Cresselley mouthed under her breath.

"We're just out of shape," Robin wisely falsified. "Think we'll take a break and unpack."

"Your gram stocked the fridge, in case you're hungry, she's so thoughtful."

The girls didn't have much of an appetite, but each grabbed a bottle of water on their way up the stairs.

"I'm going to lie down for a while," Cresselley admitted.

Robin nodded and headed into the smaller room.

*****

When Cresselley woke up, it was four o'clock in the afternoon, and her stomach was objecting loudly to the omission of lunch. She got up and peeked around the hall corner to see if Robin was awake. To her surprise, her twin was sitting cross-legged on her bed with the framed regional map from the wall on her lap.

"Oh, this looks like trouble. Planning our next adventure, sis? How did you get Dad's area map off the wall?"

"Easy," Robin brushed it off, "it just hangs on a nail. Here, El, come look at this. See, here's the Chapman Cemetery at the top of the hill. Remember, Dad has taken us there to explore several times."

"Mom too," Cresselley added softly.

"Sorry, Mom too, but look at the map just behind the tombstones. See how this old logging road heads off to the northwest. It looks like it intercepts the trail we take to the bear cave, before that path joins the blue trail to the north. Can you visualize that?"

"Oh sure," Cresselley responded sarcastically, but Robin took no heed.

"What if we get up early, so Carol doesn't question our plans, hike up to the cemetery, and go through the woods to the bear cave that way? It would be fun, El, and we'd have a new way to the cave that we could show Dad after he takes us to the Crossroads, like he promised."

"Well, when you put it that way…"

"Awesome, I'll put some gear in my backpack and you can put together some snacks to bring. It shouldn't take us more than two or three hours, depending on how overgrown the old logging road is. This will be good to get our minds off lake issues until we see Gram."

Cresselley couldn't argue with that rationalization. "Okay, Marco Polo, can we get something to eat now? My stomach is growling."

"You bet, then why don't we look through the family DVD collection and make it a movie night."

"As long as it isn't a murder mystery or a disaster flick, I'm game."

Cresselley set about making blueberry muffins for dessert and to pack for the next morning. The tempting aroma pulled Robin from the rack of DVDs and into the kitchen.

"How about this one?" Robin held up the cover so her sister could see it

"'Fly Away Home,' that's a great choice. Mom loved that film. How old were we when she first let us watch it with her?"

"Six, maybe, she was afraid we'd cry in the beginning when the mom is killed in a car crash and the daughter wakes up without her in a hospital room."

"Well, she was right, but we weren't the only ones with tears. Mom was just as moved, even though she'd seen it before, and Dad walked out of the room." Cresselley chuckled at the memory.

After dinner, Carol joined the girls in front of the aging TV. It had been a fixture in the living room for as long as either one of the twins could remember.

"No wonder this was one of Mom's favorites, I forgot there's environmental activists in it and a happy ending," Robin observed as the credits scrolled across the screen. She stood up, stretched, and announced "bedtime," winking at Cresselley.

"We're going hiking early, Carol," she added. "We need to get into shape if we are going to survive the summer."

At the top of the stairs, she addressed her sister, "I'll wake you up at six. We should make the cemetery by 6:45 or so."

Cresselley yawned and nodded.

Encounter in the Graveyard

The June sun was already up and waiting when the girls put on their backpacks and headed out through the screen door and up the driveway to the paved road. It was a lovely, warm morning and the girls had shaken off all apprehensions from the previous day. It was a short walk to the steep incline leading high above the lake with nothing but state forest on either side of the road. The morning air was filled with the intoxicating smell of pine trees and early summer wildflowers.

They turned in at the crest of the hill where the Chapman Cemetery lay a short distance down a narrow gravel path with grass growing in the middle. As the headstones came into view, the sisters were startled by the sound of something sizable approaching through the dense trees. Their father had always assured them that the "bear cave" had never actually housed bears but neither twin was inclined to take comfort in that admission at the moment. They stood their ground tensely, shoulder to shoulder, as the rustling grew louder and nearer. A minute that seemed like an hour later, a tall, handsomely attired, young man with a backpack, pushed through the undergrowth. He was just as startled to encounter the twins as they were him.

"Hi," Robin offered, visibly relieved. "What on earth, are you doing dressed like that, in the woods, at this hour of the morning?"

The young man laughed. "Yeah. I'm sure this looks fishy, but you're a surprise to me too."

"So you're bird-watching?" Cresselley teasingly speculated.

"Oh, no, sorry. I wasn't dodging the question. I'm saving the bus driver a mile and a half of road time. I take a shortcut from my house through the woods in decent weather and come out at the turnaround for the town buses at the end of the path. I'm Jesse, by the way."

"I'm Robin Spenser, and this is my sister, Cresselley."

"Wait a minute, you're still in school?" Cresselley backtracked. "We got out a week ago."

"Yeah, well, I go to the tech middle school in Northrop. We had a lot more snow days than you did, that is if you go here in North Milltown."

"We're going into the eighth grade here in the fall," Cresselley explained. "We moved with our dad from Darien around Christmastime."

"You're both going to be eighth graders, how's that?"

"You mean, did one of us repeat a grade?" Robin alleged with a smirk.

"Well, I didn't mean to pry, but—"

"We're twins," Cresselley jumped in.

"But you barely look like sisters," the young man observed.

"Everybody says that," Robin assured him. "We're fraternal twins, about five minutes apart."

"Duh." Jesse laughed. "Hey, I think my dad and I did some work for your father last fall on a house at the end of Stillman Road. Is that where you live now?"

"That's it," Robin said enthusiastically.

"We're staying in our grandmother's lake cottage with a twenty-year-old companion for the summer," Elly added. "What kind of work does your father do?"

"He's an electrician, and he's determined that I'll be one too. That's why I have to go to the tech school, though the whole thing is a pain. I'm going into the seventh grade in the fall."

Suddenly, a thought popped into Robin's head. "Jesse, do you know anything about the house that burned down off the Pentway at the lake?"

"Yeah, it was all hush-hush. The FBI and I think Homeland Security were investigating. The only reason I know is because some agent asked my dad to look at what was left of the house to rule out an electrical fire." Jesse suddenly looked toward the end of the path. "Gotta go. I hear my bus struggling up the hill. Hey, tomorrow's the last day of school, so we get out early. I'll be getting off the bus here about one o'clock if you want to meet. I know more about the fire. It's the Barkers' place you mean, right?"

"That's the one, we'll be here."

"Awesome, then you can tell me what the two of you were doing here at this hour of the morning as you put it."

The girls watched Jesse disappear down the dirt path. They heard the distinctive sound of the bus doors opening and closing. It turned around where Jesse had predicted, and though it wasn't visible from their position, the twins clearly heard it retreating down the steep grade. They looked at each other without speaking for a few minutes. Robin broke the silence.

"Wouldn't it be cool to have a new friend? Maybe he'd like to go kayaking with us?"

"I have a feeling his father keeps him pretty busy, but we can ask. Still want to explore another trail to the bear cave?"

"For sure, it's what we came for, and what a windfall for getting here early."

Robin led the way past the graveyard into the woods where she estimated from the map that the trail would begin. She was right about the location, and the trail was much more passable than either girl had envisioned.

"I thought it'd be all overgrown," Cresselley admitted. "Dad said there hasn't been any logging up here in decades."

"That's what I figured too," her guide agreed. "Maybe the state or even the town keeps it clear as a fire trail. It would be awful if a forest fire hit here. Either way, it sure makes our expedition a lot easier."

The woods were still, except for the sound of birds serenading, the girls decided to join in.

"Hey, Robbie, let's sing Mom's camp songs. How about the 'Old Caravan,' one she taught us?"

"You start," Robin agreed.

"When I was a camper in Old Caravan, my home was near by the lake…"

Robin chimed in and the two continued the song together. They made good time along the trail, until it began to slope sharply downhill, a clear indication the lake and the intercepting path they sought were near.

"Look, Elly, here it is, the route to the bear cave, I recognize that rock outcrop. We're better than halfway to it."

"You're right, I know where we are now." Cresselley was always impressed with her sister's sense of direction and navigation skills.

The girls turned right, up the winding, deeply wooded path. It only took about fifteen minutes for them to reach the turnoff. They easily recognized it through the numerous adventures to the spot with their father every summer since they were big enough to walk that far with periodic, alternating intervals on his capable shoulders. They were aware of the No Trespassing signs at the beginning of the access means, but their father explained to them early on, permission granted him by the trustee of the property, a client of his firm. This was a relationship for which the members of the Lake Association were keenly grateful. If the extensive acreage in the trust were ever sold, the environmental effects of development would bring disastrous consequences for the precious body of water.

"Looks like we're not the only 'trespassers' around here," Cresselley noted as they approached the opening to the cave. "Look at all this trash—empty cans, a pizza box, junk food wrappers—what a mess."

"I know litterers are a pet peeve of yours, sis, but come look at this." Robin was beckoning from just inside the opening of the cave.

It was dark, but there were clear signs more than one person had been "camping out" in the marginally roomy interior. Cresselley joined Robin as she pulled out and switched on a small flashlight their father insisted they bring on every outing.

"Are those sleeping bags?"

"Looks like four of them," Robin estimated, "and backpacks against the far wall."

"Why on earth would anyone want to sleep in here, unless they're doing research on spiders?"

"Or bats," Robin added.

"Let's get out of here." Though Robin didn't seem to notice, Cresselley was uneasy. "I, for one, don't want to be anywhere around when they come back and it sure looks like they have every intention of doing just that."

"You go. I'll be right behind you. I just want a quick look over…"

"Robin Elizabeth, get your butt moving!" Cresselley was trying to sound authoritarian, but her voice was quivering.

Robin looked up and finally recognized just how anxious her twin was.

"Sorry, sorry," she emerged, stepped into the daylight, and patted Cresselley's back reassuringly.

Resuming the lead, Robin immediately paced a rapid retreat down the path toward the legitimately occupied north end of the lake. She could hear her twin close on her heals and the sigh of relief she breathed as the playful sounds of several kids in the "soon to be" mid-morning summer day. As they passed the "No Trespassing" sign at the entrance, a game of "make a big splash jumping off the dock" came into view, bringing a sense of secure normalcy. The girls waved as they passed the group which appeared to be a birthday celebration, judging by the balloons.

"Seems awfully early in the day for a birthday party," Cresselley remarked.

"You know what? I bet it's a slumber birthday party that started yesterday. Remember when we had one in Darien? What were we? Seven, eight?"

Cresselley relaxed at the memory. "We had a *Frozen* theme. I was Elsa, and you were Anna, and the guests got to pick what character they wanted to be. Aya made the cutest Olaf, and Mom put so much work into the costumes and the cake.

"And Dad actually made it home from work on time. He was such a goofy Sven."

"He sure was." Cresselley chuckled. "His antlers kept falling off."

Mrs. Chapman was at the side of her house, weeding the flower beds, her huge hat dwarfing the rest of her kneeling figure. The girls did not disturb her but continued down the dead-end lane toward the paved road they'd begun the day on. They passed the little neglected A-frame, isolated from the cluster of houses the girls had just passed at the end. They had always lightheartedly referred to it as the "Halloween" house. It had a steep roofline with barely enough space at the top for one tiny window and two slightly larger ones just below it. The resulting structural design looked like watchful eyes following the twins whenever they passed. The first time their father walked them by, the daughters begged to peek in the front windows from the porch, but on closer inspection by their protective parent, the deck boards were rotting and full of holes. He did lift them up one by one to peek in the side kitchen porthole, but the glass was too opaque to reveal much of the interior. The overall ambiance of the property was further enhanced by the solicitous sign still nailed to a tree in the overgrown front yard. Weather had faded the letters but it was still legible, "Psychic Palm Readings. No appointment necessary." Today, the little house presented more of a sinister facade than a mystical one as the girls hurried by. They passed the lane's first houses and were approaching the formidable dam, when the sound of horse hooves on the pavement behind them got their attention.

"Oh, look, Robbie, it's Nancy and Pumpkin with the cart."

"Hello, Spenser twins! It's wonderful to see you again this summer. How about a lift to your grandmother's cottage?"

"Really?" Cresselley exclaimed with excitement. "We don't want to burden Pumpkin."

"Pumpkin could pull the three of us and a dozen cement blocks. Hop on up, girls, one on either side of me, unless someone would care to drive."

"This is so cool," Robin declared. "What kind of a pony is Pumpkin, Nancy?"

"He's a Haflinger, they make wonderful drivers. Is Carol staying with you again?" Nancy asked politely.

"Yes," Cresselley responded. "We adore her. How is your younger son?

"Billy? Fine, he just finished his freshman year at ECSU. You might bump into him on the lake during his day off from Stop and Shop. He and his dad, Mark, have taken up paddle boarding. I guess that's the latest craze."

"And your older son?" Cresselley continued politely. "So sorry, I don't remember his name."

"Elliott," Nancy smiled. "He and his wife Clarice live in Queens. They are very civic-minded, just like your precious mother was."

"Dad took us to Queens once. He had a client who owned an Egyptian restaurant there. The food was fantastic! Just curious, Nancy," Robin saw an opportunity. "Do you know why the boat launch is closed?"

"No, I'm just as baffled as you are. There was a lot of unusual activity on the Pentway this winter, which also puzzled me. Pumpkin and I noticed multiple tracks in the snow down the Barkers' long driveway, though the couple usually visit their children during the holidays and January. They might have someone check on the house while they are out of town. I admit, I was suspicious, and I still haven't seen the Barkers since before Christmas. Well, here we are, girls. Stop by for a visit when you can. My mare is going to give birth any day now."

"Thanks, Nancy," the twins chimed, giving Pumpkin a pat on his soft nose as they departed.

Walking down the cottage's welcoming driveway, Robin turned to her sister. "She obviously doesn't know about the fire, which confirms what we suspected about the lake community being kept in the dark.

"You're right, of course, I'm just so glad she stopped." Cresselley sighed with relief. "Nancy and Pumpkin are so down to earth."

There was a note from Carol on the dining area table, "Invited next door to brunch by Mrs. Mote. Back soon." The girls were grateful for the interlude, it gave them time to agree on a distracting project. Cresselley grabbed an orange from the bowl on the table and headed upstairs.

"I'm just going to change and check for ticks, I'm not abandoning you," she reassured Robin halfway to the second floor. "I'm open to suggestions. We need to do something productive."

"I agree, and I have an idea that will impress Grammy." Robin had no intention of changing her clothes; besides, her present outfit was perfect if her sister went along with her proposal.

"Okay, I'm listening." Cresselley sat at the top of the stairs, exchanging her hiking boots for sneakers.

"Well, you might want a smock," Robin observed.

"Why, are we cooking?"

"Painting," Robin clarified. "Remember, Grammy hinted the exteriors of the two windows where Carol sleeps need a fresh coat?"

"Great idea! Does Gram have primer and enough Benjamin Moore Cottage red?"

"Everything we need is in the cabinet under the life jackets. Bummer, we have to start with a little scrapping." Robin actually enjoyed painting trim, but the prep work was unrewarding.

The girls collected the materials and Cresselley went into the kitchen to find a suitable apron. Robin dragged two stools to the side of the house and put one squarely under each of the bedroom windows.

"South or West?" Robin offered her twin the choice of windows.

"Whichever this one is," Cresselley announced as she mounted the stool on the driveway side of the cottage. "Hand me a wire brush, will you? There's a bunch of cruds on the sill."

The girls finished the prep work and were about halfway through the priming stage when they heard the bang of the screen door on the front porch.

"Carol's back," Robin whispered. "You know she'll be in here in a minute fussing with her hair and makeup. Follow my lead, I have a great stunt in mind."

Robin squatted down so that she could just peek into the little bedroom and Cresselley imitated her. Just as the girls suspected, Carol came in and sat in front of the little vanity mirror. Robin was perfectly still until Carol took her eyes off her reflection, rummaging for mascara. Robin cleverly took advantage of Carol's distraction and positioned her head in the window so that her own face was visible in the mirror. When Carol glanced back at her image, there was Robin's contorted face staring at her. She screamed, turned around quickly to confront the trickster, and slid off the chair with a bump on the floor. For a brief moment, Robin considered she might have gone a little too far this time, but Carol dusted herself off and grinned.

"Okay, you two, you got me, happy?"

Robin nodded.

"What on earth are you standing in the windows for anyway? I assume you're on stools and haven't grown a foot since yesterday."

Cresselley held up her paintbrush. "We're giving your windows a makeover." She chuckled.

"Well, aren't you considerate? When you can take a break, I want to show the both of you something Mrs. Mote gave me."

"Hey, how was brunch?" Robin asked politely.

"So good." Carol patted her abdomen. "I don't need to eat for another week."

"We'll be in ten minutes tops."

The girls were dying with curiosity but refrained from asking premature questions.

"I'll be in the recliner on the porch, digesting," Carol called behind her as she left the little room.

The girls quickly finished with the primer, dropped their paintbrushes in a can of water, and joined the already dozing Carol.

"Boo," Cresselley teased and Carol sat up straight in the recliner.

"Okay, so when your dad was making arrangements for me to move in with you for the summer vacation, he was very clear that he didn't want you…us hanging out here all of the time. He wants you or us to do some 'fun' things and some 'educational' activities. I want suggestions from you, and I have a few ideas of my own."

"Does this have anything to do with a gift from Mrs. Mote?" Cresselley inquired patiently.

"As a matter of fact, it does. She gave me a flyer with the local schedule for summer things to do"—Carol paused deliberately—"Guess what's playing tomorrow night at our favorite movie venue?"

"You mean the Shore Road drive-in?"

The girls loved the outdoor theater and the selections they showed. It was a summer tradition with their parents when they joined the girls vacationing with their grandmother.

"Yes, now guess!"

"*Jaws*," Cresselley offered.

"July 15," Carol checked the schedule.

"How about *Ferris Bueller's Day Off.*" Robin hated guessing games.

Carol shook her head.

"*Titanic.*" Cresselley knew they wouldn't get an answer unless they guessed correctly or if Carol gave in.

"August 5, one more each and I'll tell you."

"Dad's favorite…" Robin went first. "*To Kill a Mockingbird.*"

"It's playing on July 29. That's a Saturday. Maybe your dad would like to take you," Carol suggested optimistically.

"And the last guess is…"—Cresselley mimicked a drum roll—"*Jurassic Park.*"

"*Ghostbusters.*" Carol laughed cheerfully.

"We love that movie!" Robin was genuinely enthusiastic.

"I know you do. So how about this?" Carol recommended. "We leave about seven o'clock, pick up grinders in the village, and eat at the picnic tables there. The film starts at eight thirty, so you girls can have time on the swings before it begins if you aren't too grown up for that this summer."

"Sounds perfect," Cresselley complimented.

"Can we invite a friend?" Robin surprised mostly Carol.

"Sure," Carol agreed. "Who'd you have in mind?"

"We met this boy, Jesse, on our hike this morning. He's a year younger than we are," Robin explained.

"Dad knows his father," Cresselley added, "and he probably met Jesse at least once too. His dad is the electrician who worked on the Stillman Road house before we moved in. Jesse goes to the tech school because his dad wants him to be an electrician too."

"Wow, you learned a lot in one encounter," Carol observed. "He sounds like a great kid. Where does he live?"

"The last house on the road, right on the edge of the state forest," Robin answered. "His last half day of school is tomorrow, and we agreed to meet him when he gets off the bus at one o'clock. We can ask him then."

"I'm sure your dad will be pleased you've made a new friend. If he gets permission and wants to join us, let him know we can pick him up at about six forty-five," Carol volunteered. "And let him know about dinner on the grounds."

The girls were relieved Carol didn't ask if they had walked all the way to the end of the road. They weren't crazy about admitting going through the graveyard entrance to the bear cave. The less she knew about their discoveries and jaunts in the woods, the better.

"Hey, Carol," Robin teased, "how about some lunch?"

Carol groaned but grinned. "You girls knock yourselves out. Do you have plans for this afternoon?"

"We're going to finish sprucing up your windows," Cresselley stated resolutely, heading for the kitchen.

After lunch, back on their painting stools, Robin addressed her twin with a serious tone.

"Elly, we need to be in agreement how much we share with Jesse about our findings in the bear cave this morning."

"We need to agree on what we stumbled on in the bear cave this morning," Cresselley insisted. "We don't know who those people are or why they're on the property. I mean it could be legitimate. Maybe they're researching by request of the trustee. You know, studying the effects of climate change on the enormous standing pines for example."

"Now you sound like Mom and as I recall, you weren't all that keen on waiting around to ask them the purpose of their cave occupation."

"I know," Cresselley sounded apologetic, "but should we just let our imaginations run wild?"

"You're right, sis, let's consider what we've discovered so far, find out what more Jesse can add tomorrow, and go from there."

"That's alarmingly sensible," Cresselley confirmed. "If Jesse has more to say about the investigation of the fire, that might be related to the boat launch and whatever is going on at the cave, we'll tell him everything."

"Pinkie swear?" Robin held up her little finger.

"Pinkie swear."

Just as they were finishing the painting project, Robin got her twin's attention. "El, you hear that?"

"Hear what?"

"Outboards, big ones, I bet the boat launch is back open. Let's suit up and take out the kayaks."

The girls waved to Carol on the dock and launched into the midafternoon commotion on the lake. Robin was right, there were almost a dozen motorboats noisily pulling water-skiers, tubes full of screaming kids, and brave wakeboarders. The churning water lapped sizable waves against the girls' rocking kayaks, much to their delight.

"Here comes a big one." Cresselley beamed over at Robin, paddling fiercely through the maelstrom.

It took almost twice their usual time to come into sight of the boat launch but there was no doubt, the cones blocking the state access were gone. The girls bobbed along on the churning surface of the lake enjoying the ample company; and the scene so transformed from barely a week ago.

Jesse

The following morning, Cresselley woke to the gentle "pitter-patter" of rain on the cottage roof. She tapped lightly on the thin wall above her head. Robin's bed was just on the other side. A soft knock was returned. Cresselley slid out of bed and around the corner into her sister's room.

"It's raining," she announced grimly.

"We like the occasional rainy morning here," Robin reminded her visitor.

"But not today." Cresselley was perceptibly disappointed.

Robin shrugged her shoulders.

"Remember what Jesse said, he takes the shortcut on 'decent' days."

"I think he was referring to not snowing or ten degrees," Robin pointed out, "and it might clear up by the time we leave. Either way, if we get there, he'll see us and get off the bus."

"You're right. It's just that…we don't even know his last name."

"But Dad does and we know where he lives," Robin reminded. "Stop worrying, we can eat breakfast, do some chores, pack lunch for three, and go."

Cresselley looked relieved and went back across the hall to get dressed. It was still lightly raining after breakfast. Robin put a towel over head and went to check on yesterday's paint job. Fortunately, the trim had dried before the rain began and the windows looked great. At noon, the girls headed up the same route they'd taken the previous morning. The sky was clearing and the day was shaping up to be another beauty.

"Do you think he forgot about us?"

"Elly, stop," Robin instructed. "You're making me nuts."

The girls didn't wait long before they heard the bus climbing the hill. It stopped right next to them and out stepped a grinning Jesse.

"Hey, you're here." He was authentically pleased as he crossed the road to greet them. "Let's see, Robin and Cresselley, right?"

"Right, how was your last day of school?" Cresselley asked politely.

"So glad to be out," Jesse admitted. "Of course, summer will be mostly working for my dad. Oh well, at least he pays me. Can you wait for a second? There's something I need to do right away."

The twins glanced at each other, wondering if they should turn their backs as Jesse disappeared into the bushes he had so mysteriously appeared from the morning before. They didn't wonder long. There was a loud whistle and a second later Jesse re-emerged with a big, sandy colored animal.

"A doggo!" The girls were enchanted.

"She's good," Jesse reassured. "Aren't you, girl? You waited patiently for me all morning."

"We love dogs. Dad keeps promising us, but our companion during the school year doesn't like animals in the house," Robin said with regret.

"Well, this is Acey. My Dad has her brother to guard the truck and valuable equipment when he's on a job. You wouldn't believe how many times he was robbed before he got DC."

Robin laughed. "ACDC… You realize how lame that would be for two electricians if it weren't so ingenious."

"It was my dad's idea, but we like it, don't we, girl?" Jesse fondly scratched behind the dog's ears.

"Are you hungry, we packed a picnic," Cresselley offered.

"Man, I could eat," Jesse confessed. "I'm in the eleven thirty lunch group, and of course, we didn't have a regular schedule today, I'm starving."

"Great," the twin took a drop cloth from her bag, and together, the girls set out an appetizing spread.

"Sorry, we don't have anything for Acey," Robin apologized.

"No worries"—the dog's affectionate owner dug in his backpack and withdrew a large dog treat—"Here, girl, lie down."

The dog lay contentedly about a foot from her owner, never taking her eyes off him as he devoured a tuna and tomato sandwich.

"Wow, thanks, this is great. Are those blueberry muffins?" Jesse eagerly eyed the next course.

"Help yourself!" Cresselley encouraged, "We have Georgia peaches too."

The girls truly enjoyed watching the young man eat with such abandon.

"Sorry, I know you want to hear more about the fire"—Jesse licked peach juice off his fingers and leaned forward—"So this agent or whatever he was came to see my dad for his report on the wiring after dinner one night. I was in my room doing homework. I could tell they were having a discussion, but I couldn't make out the words. I confess, I hid at the top of the stairs and listened. They were having beers, which might have made the conversation a little less 'tight-lipped,' so to speak. The guy was telling my dad how his agency had been watching the Barkers' house with suspicion for about a week. He didn't say exactly why, but I got the impression, it was being used as part of some illegal activity under investigation. Apparently, the assumption about the fire was arson, like the crew was onto being watched and needed to destroy any and all evidence fast. I know how crazy this all sounds, especially in this town where rolling through a stop sign is the most serious crime on the books, but maybe that's the point. Whoever these dudes are probably realize how unlikely their detection would be in such a setting. And let's face it, the lake is mostly unoccupied off season. Who would notice them crashing at the Barkers'?"

The girls listened, captivated by Jesse's narrative, but waited for him to finish before commenting.

"So finally," he continued, "the detective or agent, I guess he was, asked my dad if he had noticed any unfamiliar vehicles around the lake or in town recently. I almost fell down the stairs when he said 'yes, he had'. My dad went on to tell this guy how driving home late one night from a job on Babcock Road, this van he didn't recognize sped out of the Pentway and practically forced him off the road. It was too dark to see the driver, but he was sure it was out of state plates, possibly New York."

"Did closing the boat launch happen around the same time?" Robin asked. "Oh, and guess what, it reopened yesterday."

"It did happen at the same time, and great about the launch. My dad has a little Boston Whaler we like to put in there."

"Can you think of any reason why the two incidences might be related?" Cresselley was just as curious.

"I thought about it at the time, especially since it was the beginning of fishing season. All I could come up with was the investigators didn't want people on the water with access to the scene."

"So do you think it's a closed case now or everybody's just laying low?" Robin sought Jesse's opinion.

"I don't have much to back it up, but I doubt anything is resolved, and I bet that gang, whatever it is they're up to, just went deeper underground. Okay, now it's your turn," Jesse addressed the twins, "what were *you* doing here at such an early hour yesterday?"

The girls looked at each other, silently agreeing it was time to tell Jesse what they had discovered.

Robin began. "We were pretty upset after all the weird stuff going on at the lake, so we decided to look for the old logging road up here and see if we could follow it to the intercepting path that leads to the bear cave. Have you ever been to the cave, Jesse?"

"My dad took me once. I think I was six."

"Our dad takes us every year, so we wanted to surprise him with a different route. Well, we found it no problem and quicker than we thought." Robin continued with the events of yesterday, pausing briefly to answer Jesse's questions.

"So what do you think?" the girls asked him when Robin was finished, "harmless stuff or foul play? We don't want to jump to conclusions."

"You're right about that, my imagination has a big pull. My parents limit screen time so I read a lot of mystery novels and play music."

"Our dad limits us too, there's no Wi-Fi in the cottage. Cresselley is the big reader," Robin admitted, "though my head gets pretty active."

"She watches a lot of cop-and-lawyer shows on the weekends," Cresselley teased.

"So why don't we agree to wait and see," Jesse suggested. "We know the authorities are investigating. If we discover anything more, we can always go to Officer Mendez in his town hall unit."

"That's reasonable," Robin approved, "and in the meantime, we'll ask our dad to see if the trustee for the land has given permission for any projects on the property."

"Solid"—Jesse grinned—"let's move on to something else, how about dead people? Have you ever looked at the headstones here?"

"Oh yes," Cresselley said enthusiastically, "all of them. The stones tell stories or rather family histories."

"Are they all Chapman's?" Jesse asked with curiosity.

"Mostly. The wives are from other generational dynasties in town, like Wheeler, Miner, Palmer, Babcock, you know…roads."

"Where should I start? Give me a suggestion here, girls."

"See the small one just to your left," Cresselley jumped in.

"This?" Jesse was skeptical. "Isn't this a foot stone?"

"Read it," the twin instructed.

"Infant," Jesse kneeled and read out loud. "Born August 12, 1856. Lived one day. Oh, that's grim."

"Infant mortality," Robin explained, "now the big one next to it."

"Rachael Gallup Chapman. Hey, I know the Gallops, big farm on the town line, Wife of Elijah S. Chapman. Born September 23, 1838. Died August 12, 1856. She was so young," Jesse observed. "Wait a minute, the baby's mom?"

"Maternal mortality, pretty common back then. Keep going."

"Let's see, Elijah S. Chapman. Born January 3, 1828. Died March 14, 1888. Beloved Husband: Rest in Peace. So the dude lived to be sixty. Beloved husband, but his wife died, who buried this guy?"

"One more." The girls were amused by Jesse's perplexity.

"Mary Stedman Chapman. Wife of Elijah S. Chapman. Born May 15, 1839. Died July 6, 1895. I get it, wife number two, and she outlived him. He sure liked the young ones, didn't he? Any more dead kids in this family?"

"If there were any, they're not here. They could have had girls who married and ended up in one of the other 156 graveyards in town," Cresselley speculated.

"That many? Wow!" Jesse was impressed with the girl's knowledge. "Are these veterans with the flags, they look brand-new."

"The boy scouts put new ones on all the vets in town for Memorial Day every year," Cresselley explained.

Jesse stepped back to read the nearest engraving and almost fell over Acey.

"Hey girl, chill. I'm not going anywhere without you. What's the matter, graveyards creep you out? Well, if this guy fought in a war, it must have been the war of 1812. Hey, all these Chapmans out here in the woods with nothing around. If this is a family cemetery, where did they all live?"

"Right here," Robin explained, "You see all the stone walls? They marked off fields and farmland at one time. Jesse, you've been in the woods, have you ever noticed the old foundations scattered about?"

"You know, I have and never really thought about it," the young man admitted. "What happened to the farms and the people?"

"During FDR's 'new deal' the land was purchased from the owners and turned into the state forest it is today." Cresselley continued, "The houses and outbuildings were typically burned down."

"Oh man, do I feel bad," Jesse remarked. "I love history, but I didn't know any of that and I've lived here my whole life."

"Don't feel bad," Robin reassured him, "we wouldn't know any of it either if it weren't for our gram and dad, who grew up here."

"But my dad moved here when he was ten, and he never told me any of it. In fact, I'm pretty sure our dads not only knew each other but graduated together."

"That reminds us, Jesse, what's your last name?"

"Bostick," Jesse answered and then added, "My dad's name is Kami. Everybody calls him Kam."

Suddenly, Acey began barking with insistence.

"What is it, girl, a squirrel?"

But the dog was standing over something in the tall grass that apparently was not moving.

"What ya got there?" Jesse bent down and picked up the offending object."

"What is it?" the girls were curious.

"It's a New York Yankees cap," Jesse replied. "Can't have been here long, it's not wet from this morning's showers. That's odd," he added so softly as to be barely audible.

"What is?" Robin came up from behind for a look. "I swear I smell perfume or flowery shampoo on it."

"Hey," Cresselley scolded. "Girls can have a favorite team and wear logos."

"Sure, but have you ever seen anyone around this graveyard? In all the times I've taken my shortcut, I have never seen any evidence of another visitor except for the flags." Jesse looked perplexed.

"Who knows, maybe one of the Chapmans paid their respects." Cresselley brushed it off.

"You're right." Jesse relaxed. "Guess I'm getting paranoid. What is it now, girl? Finders keepers, want the hat?" Getting hungry maybe?" Jesse glanced at his phone. "No wonder, can't believe it's almost three o'clock. Okay, we're going in just a minute."

Robin and Cresselley were equally amazed at the time.

Changing the topic, Robin grinned. "We almost forgot. Would you like to go to the Shore Road Drive-In Theater with us tonight? It's short notice, but we just found out that *Ghostbusters* is playing."

"You want me to go?" Jesse relaxed his frown. "Is it okay with your, what do you call her, companion?"

"Carol thinks it's a great idea and Dad's treating," Cresselley informed their new friend. "Do you think your parents will let you come?"

"I don' see why not, we're almost neighbors. How are 'bars' at the lake?"

"Dreadful," Robin admitted. "The only reliable spot is the end of the dock. Give me your phone. I'll put our numbers in it. What time do you want to text us?"

"My mom should be home in an hour… How about five on the dot, on the dock?"

"Great." Cresselley clapped her hands. "Wait, what about Acey? Won't she miss you?"

"Naw, she hangs out with DC after dinner."

"Carol says, if you can come, we'll pick you up at 6:45."

"Oh, and we'll have a picnic dinner on the grounds," Cresselley added.

"Cool, two picnics in one day." Jesse called over his shoulder as Acey led him toward home.

Halfway down the hill, Robin had a thought. "Hey Elly, you know that box in the crawl space with Dad's old books in it?"

"It's still there?" Cresselley questioned.

"It is. Let's drag it out when we get back. I'm pretty sure Dad's senior yearbook is in it. We can look up Jesse's father."

The girls dashed upstairs to Robin's room the minute they burst through the door. Robin drew back the curtain, concealing the roomy crawl space in the low roofline over the cottage's well-designed kitchen.

"Here, Elly, grab it." Robin was forced to bend uncomfortably at the waist to clear the ceiling as she pushed the book box ahead of her.

"Got it!"

The girls blew away the dust and peered inside.

"This could be it," Cresselley held up a flat volume with the local school's mascot on the cover.

"Look at the year."

"1987."

"Not it," Robin answered. "Mom and Dad graduated in 1988. Here's another one. Oh man, this is it."

Together, the girls leafed through the pages. There were notes and signatures from classmates as well as teachers.

"Here's Mom, we've seen this before, and Dad, what a hairdo."

"Go to the *B*s, Robbie, *Bostick*," Jesse said.

"Here he is, Kami Nzabonimana Bostick. That's a tongue twister of a middle name." Cresselley looked over Robin's shoulder to the print under the picture. She read: "cross-country, class vice president junior year, shop club, well that makes sense and look here, Robbie"—Cresselley pointed to the page—"band and chorus, a musician. Remember Jesse said he reads mysteries and plays music? What if instead of listening to music, he meant playing an instrument?"

"I didn't take it that way either," Robin confided. "We'll have to ask him."

The girls silently read the rest of the entry for Jesse's dad and sat on the bed stunned. Who would have imagined the reason Mr. Bostick moved here when he was ten? The yearbook starkly revealed that Jesse's paternal grandparents had perished in the Rwandan genocide in 1994, and his orphaned father had been adopted by the Bostick family in town through a Christian organization.

"I wonder if that's why Jesse is interested in history," Cresselley queried out loud. "We'll have to be sensitive if we decide to talk to him about any of this, but I'm glad we found out."

"I'm with you on that," Robin agreed.

"Hey, what time is it?" Cresselley suddenly sat up straight on the bed.

"Fluffy bunnies, it's five minutes to five," Robin consulted her Fitbit. "We gotta get to the dock pronto."

The girls sprinted out the porch door, sidestepped Carol on the wooden platform, and turned on their phones. Three minutes later, a brief text came through on Robin's screen. "6:45" was all it read.

"It's official, Carol, we're four," she informed the startled sunbather. "We're going to wash up and find something to wear."

Carol wanted so badly to comment on Robin volunteering to change her clothes but thought better of it.

The Shore Road Drive-In

At 6:30, the little Prius and its three passengers took off for the end of the road. Jesse and his parents were waiting on the lawn of the pretty little cape. The young man made polite introductions and everyone shook hands.

"Thank you, girls, for inviting our sixth-grade graduate to the drive-in." Mrs. Bostick smiled. "I'm afraid with our work schedules, we don't get out very often. This is a generous treat."

"We're glad we bumped into each other yesterday," the girls responded sincerely.

"Say hello to your dad for me"—Mr. Bostick smiled at the twins—"Tell him I'd like to get together when he's in town."

"For sure," the girls reassured.

"I'll have him home by 11:00," Carol promised the couple as they waved goodbye through the car windows.

Ten minutes later, they turned into the sole takeout eatery in town.

"I'm taking grinder orders," Carol announced.

"A regular, no bologna, Swiss cheese on onion bread," Robin was quick to select.

"Ditto." Jesse grinned.

"And the food critic?" Carol looked at Cresselley in the rearview mirror.

"I'll have vegetarian with Italian dressing on wheat."

"Two and two, perfect. Be here when I get back." Carol grinned and stepped out into the parking lot.

The minute she was out of earshot, Jesse addressed the girls.

"I couldn't wait to talk to you," he said in a low tone. "I thought of something else that might be linked, after we went home this afternoon, and the appearance of the Yankees cap. Last Saturday night, Dad and I worked late as usual. When we left the job, it must have been around midnight. As we passed the entrance to the graveyard, I noticed taillights right about where we ate lunch. I figured, you know 'potheads' or punks doing who knows what, but after you told me about the trail and the bear cave, I remembered something else. The lights went out as we passed, not surprising, but just before it went dark, the headlights seemed like they were pointed in a precise direction, like looking for something or even signaling. I didn't think anything of it at the time, but now..." Jesse's voice trailed off.

"All together, these events can't be mere coincidence," Robin surmised. "But we need some concrete evidence, not mysterious lights and trespassers. Otherwise, we just come off like a bunch of bored juveniles."

"You're right," Jesse acknowledged. "I just wish we could get in touch with that FBI agent, not that he'd pay us any attention. I wonder if they have any idea what these guys are involved with."

"The FBI steps in with interstate crimes. Dad's worked on cases like that, mostly drugs, some counterfeit passports, kidnappings. So the New York license plates make sense, otherwise it would be under Officer Mendez's jurisdiction," Robin explained.

"Man, you pick up a lot," Jesse said with admiration. "Here comes Carol," he cautioned.

"Okay, we're good." Carol slipped behind the wheel and joined the local traffic.

It was about a twenty-minute ride to the outdoor theater. All the traffic was coming at them in the opposite direction, heading home after a magnificent day at the beach.

"I'm glad we're going this way," Jesse observed. "I had no idea how much beach traffic there is!"

"It gets worse after the fourth of July," Carol mentioned. "The ocean water is still pretty chilly. We usually brave it once a summer, don't we, girls? This is the perfect time of day to come."

The little Prius turned west onto Shore Road, passed all the tourist businesses, many of which close in the off season and within minutes, approached the entrance to the outdoor theater.

"That is one awesome screen," Jesse marveled as the towering white structure came into view. "Wonder how it manages in a hurricane."

The girls giggled at Jesse's amazement.

"Have you seen *Ghostbusters*?" Carol inquired.

"No, but my mom is a big fan of Ernie Hudson and a lot of my friends like it."

The fee at the gate was $20 per car. The twins' parents had entertained them the first time they brought them to see *Mulan* with tales from their teen years of stowing classmates in the trunk, to enable the biggest carload possible. There were a few early comers taking advantage of the picnic tables and the swings, whom the four joined with their grinders and bottled water. Carol got a text from her boyfriend and excused herself from the group.

"Jesse, do you play an instrument?" Cresselley began.

"Guitar, piano, a little flute. Where did that question come from?" Jesse chuckled.

"We confess, we looked up your father in Dad's senior yearbook," Cresselley sounded a little guilty.

"It listed band and chorus under his picture," Robin added. "We thought musical ability might run in the family."

"I don't know about ability, but I definitely have the passion. Dad played the flute, but he doesn't touch it now." Jesse's face darkened. "So you know about his Rwandan heritage, I'm pretty sure that's in his profile too."

"We're sorry, we didn't mean to snoop."

"No worries, he won't talk about it, sometimes I wish he would. I know he remembers my biological grandparents."

"Grandpa Spenser was a Colonel in the Vietnam War. He died of cancer when Dad was young, but Gram says he wouldn't talk about it either," Robin sympathized. "Is he close to his adoptive parents?"

"They're great," Jesse beamed. "We do holidays and all with them. Mom grew up in Mississippi. We don't see much of her family, so Grandma and Pops Bostick are really important to us."

"Hey," Carol's voice came across the parking area, it's showtime."

The trio got up, deposited their trash, and joined her.

"You three can sit in the back and I'll sit sideways in the front. That way we can all see." Carol hung the speaker on the car door while everyone got settled.

It was such a fun movie.

At intermission, Carol handed Robin a ten-dollar bill. "Popcorn anyone?"

On the way home, the new friends talked about the summer.

"Does your dad give you a day off?" Cresselley asked.

"He does, but it's not always the same day of the week, which is a bummer for making plans."

"What if we set some specific text or call times like we did for tonight," Robin suggested.

"We can do that." Jesse was delighted. "How about every other day at five, that's easy to remember. If I don't answer right away, we're working late. Dad doesn't allow my cell on jobsites. But I'll leave a text with a good time to try again. And if you or I find out any more about, you know," Jesse whispered. "We'll get together as soon as possible."

The girls nodded in agreement as Carol turned into the driveway at the end of the road.

"Thank you, Carol, this was great," the young man expressed as Cresselley slid out of the backseat to let him out of the middle. "And thank your dad for me." He stood waving as the hybrid backed out of the driveway.

Robin Reflects

Robin woke to the sound of geese. She lifted her head off the pillow and gazed out the bedroom window. It was one of the lake's newest families—a goose, a gander, and ten baby goslings—all pecking at grass on the lawn not five feet from the porch below. The babies would be almost full grown by the time school started.

No, Robin thought to herself. *Not going to think about the fall.*

Anyway, it was a hot, humid, morning, unmistakably summer. Though Cresselley vehemently denied snoring, that is precisely what she was doing loudly on the other side of the bedroom wall. Robin felt restless and got up. Her mind was racing, mystified by the string of recent, inexplicable, events surrounding the lake. If only she could put a reasonable explanation to them or be convinced the authorities had a handle on the situation, she would let the whole thing go, but that was not the case. Robin quietly crossed the lawn, not to startle the little grazing family, and paced impatiently at the end of the dock. What could she possibly do to help get to the bottom of this mystery? Going over the string of events and the decisions the sisters had made with Jesse, suddenly, she recalled a detail the three had agreed on—ask Dad if there were authorized activities taking place on the land trust.

Excited and determined, the twin took out her phone and pulled up the law firm's landline. She might have a better chance of reaching her father directly.

The practice's charming assistant answered. "Robin," more of a statement than a question. "How are you? Do you need to talk to your dad? He's in his office, I can put you through."

Robin's hunch had paid off. Fatima was always generous when the girls phoned and their dad wasn't tied up. Robin suspected she was aware of how little they got to see him and they wouldn't phone the office unless it was of paramount importance.

"Dad, it's me," Robin immediately announced when she heard the phone pick up.

"Robbie, what's wrong?" her father sounded alarmed.

"Nothing, Dad, we're all fine."

Robert sighed with relief and quickly composed himself. "I heard you girls met Jesse Bostick and you all went to the Shore Road Drive-in last night, is that right, sweetheart?"

"Yes, Dad, and thanks for treating us." Robin hurried on, not wanting the conversation to end before she could convey the real reason behind the call. "Dad, do you know if the trustee for the land here has given permission for any kind of a project on the property?"

"Not that I've been made aware of, why? Have you girls stumbled onto something?"

"Not really, just a bunch of litter on the trail to the bear cave," Robin revealed as casually as she could.

"I worry about you girls exploring on your own," Robert remarked without placing restraints on their freedom. "I wish you would wait for me to go with you."

Sadly, he recognized the reason for silence on the other end of the line. Robin would never articulate what he knew she was thinking. For a moment, the pause hung between them.

"Honey, can you wait on the line for a minute? I'll make a call right now and get an answer for you immediately."

Robin stood still as possible on the dock to minimize the risk of losing her bars. Fortunately, she didn't wait long.

"The answer is 'no,' sweetie," her father's voice was confident. "Mr. Pendleton assures me there have been no changes to the status of the property or those with permission to access it. Shall I contact Officer Mendez and ask him to keep an eye out?"

"You can, Dad," Robin agreed, "but he might already have stepped up patrols around the lake area just because it's summer."

"That's very true, honey, but I think I'll phone him anyway. I can reassure the members of the trust that their property rights are being protected." Robin heard her father chuckling. "I'll tell Horace Pendleton my sleuthing daughters are on the case."

"Dad, please come home this weekend." Robin so wanted to confide in her father that unauthorized trash was not all his "sleuthing" daughters had discovered, but under the circumstances, it felt like blackmail.

"I'll do my best," her father promised. "Give Elly a big squeeze for me and an enormous 'Thank You' to Carol. I love you, Robbie, stay safe."

The phone clicked and once again, her father may as well have been on the moon. She hated the temptation of feeling sorry for herself. After all, Elly was in the same boat. But at that vulnerable moment, Robin truly felt like an orphan. Fighting back tears, she sat down and draped her feet in the soothing water. Aware of the dock's vibration, signaling the approach of another living being, Robin quickly dried her eyes. To her surprise, without a word, Carol sat down and tenderly enveloped her shoulders. It was more than Robin could bear. After two years of putting on a brave face, she broke down and sobbed. Carol held the young girl, patiently waiting for Robin to let out her long, suppressed grief.

When Robin finished sobbing, she looked up at Carol. "Why doesn't he want to be around us anymore?" she pleaded.

"Oh, sweetie, can't you guess?"

"Please, Carol, I really need to know. Doesn't he love us like before Mom died?"

Carol's face softened and a tear ran down her cheek. "He loves you more," she whispered.

"Then why does he have such a hard time being around us?"

"Look in the mirror, sweetheart, and at your sister. In your own way, each of you is the spitting image of your mother. Not just the way you look, but your mannerism, personality, the whole package."

Robin was puzzled by Carol's observations. "I would think that would be comforting to him, not a sad reminder."

"I know that for two years now, all of the adults in your life have advised the two of you to be patient with your dad. That as soon as he wraps up x number of important cases for the firm, he'll come home to you. I'm not going to say that exactly, you know why?"

"No," Robin admitted.

"Because for two summers, I have witnessed and felt your sadness every time he promises to come home and inescapably disappoints you. It breaks my heart, and I want to be furious at him."

"But you aren't?"

"I can't be, any more than you girls can. Everyone responds differently to great loss. Your father throws himself into work, which keeps him from you and his mounting doubt about being a good single parent. That's why he moved you near your grandmother. Do you understand, Robbie, a little, maybe?"

"He's always been a great dad." Robin didn't understand why her father might have doubts.

"As part of a team, honey"—Carol paused to give Robin time to absorb what she was suggesting before continuing—"You girls suffered a loss no child should have to endure. But your father lost not only the love of his life, but his partner…his compass. When you and Cresselley were born, your parents became matching bookends with you in the protective, loving middle. When one of the pieces is gone…" Carol didn't feel the need to finish. "Would it help to talk about your mom and how she died?"

"No, the counselor we saw for a year was good." Robin sat still for a while and then looked up with gratitude at her wise companion.

"Thank you, Carol, I get it now. I can try to be patient, like Elly," she added.

"What brought all this on?" Carol asked.

"I called his office and Fatima let me talk to him," Robin admitted.

"Well, that makes sense." Carol nodded. "He's there, you girls are here."

"I asked him to come for the weekend, he said he'd try."

"I promise you, honey, this will all be over very soon. You girls are turning thirteen in November, a fact that your dad is keenly aware of and one concept all parents fear, the teen years. Believe me, he knows the need to be on top of everything you girls do, right through to college."

Robin smiled with relief. Everything Carol told her sounded so wise and reassuring.

A vibration in the dock alerted the two that something with legs was quickly approaching. Cresselley was Robin's first thought, until a big, wet tongue slobbered her face.

"Katie, you out for a walk? Where's Judy?" she inquired while affectionately rubbing the basset hound's enormous ears.

"Here I am," a lovely, retired woman from the lake neighborhood greeted. "Kadie, you just love attention."

Carol stood up and asked Judy how she was enjoying the summer.

"This humidity keeps us from our longer walks, but we're managing, aren't we, girl?" she turned the question on her four-legged friend. "The ticks seem more insidious than ever. I've been pulling them off the two of us by the dozen."

"You're right about that," Carol affirmed. "The girls check themselves over after each outing. They have both been treated for Lyme tick disease more than once."

"It's frightening how many neighbors have been infected with it," Judy commented. "Robin, Katie knows you are a dog lover and exactly how to take advantage of your fondness."

Robin smiled and continued to pet the little dog. Just then, the slam of the porch screen door got their attention. Cresselley approached the little group, looking as though she had just woken from a one-hundred-year nap.

"What did I miss?" she inquired. "Oh, doggie time." She eagerly joined Robin on the dock.

"You girls are spoiling her so, and she loves it, but we need to get on our way, or I'll be carrying her home." Judy said her goodbyes, promising to stop by for lunch one day and give the twins plenty of time to indulge her precious companion.

"Robbie, why didn't you wake me up?" Cresselley pleaded. "You know I love Katie too."

"She just wandered over five minutes ago," Carol came to Robin's defense with a gentle tone. "Do you girls have plans for today after breakfast? It's going to be a hot, humid one."

"Food sounds like a good start," Robin confessed as she glanced over at her sister." Then maybe we can play 'think.'"

Carol smiled. She knew the game Robin was referencing. It was another cherished tradition their mother had introduced her daughters to. Following a cold breakfast even Cresselley agreed to, the twins went upstairs to make their beds.

"You should consider taking a broom to this place sometime soon," Cresselley suggested as she peeked into Robin's space. "How can you stand all of these cobwebs?"

"Not everyone is afraid of spiders," her sister responded delicately. "Sit on the bed. Do you want to play Mom's boredom solution game now?"

"Absolutely, you go first."

"Okay, how about we paint the trim on the kitchen windows?"

"Let's float around on our air mattresses," Cresselley set a less ambitious tone, "your turn."

"How about we pick early blueberries off the islands from the canoe?"

"I vote *B* and then *C*," Cresselley made her selection.

"Done," Robin conceded, "only how about changing the order before it gets any hotter?"

"I'll grab a few bowls for us and meet you on the beach," Cresselley agreed.

The Storm

The temperature and humidity were in a vertical climb as the girls paddled toward "Blueberry Island" with Robin in the stern position guiding the boat's direction. They preferred the kayaks for most outings on the lake, but the berried island was so dense with vegetation, it was impenetrable. The girls typically stood up in the canoe and picked the luscious fruit that hung over the water.

"Robbie, look, there are a few ripe ones," Cresselley declared with excitement as the bushes came into view.

The girls hung on to the branches and pulled themselves and the canoe along the shoreline as they picked. Their bowls were about halfway full when abruptly, the sky grew black and threatening. The sound of thunder was audible in the distance and the girls could see flashes of lightening just beyond the tree line, above the north end cove.

Robin addressed her twin with a firm voice, "Elly, we have to take cover immediately or we'll be in deep trouble out here on the water."

"We can't get on land here," Cresselley reminded.

"I know, we've got to make Boy Scout Island as fast as possible before that storm comes crashing down on us. Remember the little shack in the middle, we can take cover there." Robin was keenly aware she was alarming her sister, but she knew just how perilous their predicament could become in a matter of minutes.

Cresselley didn't debate, she put her back into paddling, pulling as hard as she could. The seconds between the flashes and the thunder became barely perceptible; Robin decided not to count. It wasn't a great distance to the bigger island and fortuitously, the boy scouts had made trails, but the wind was pounding the water against the side of the canoe and it was all Robin could do to keep the tiny vessel pointed in the right direction. They were within a few minutes of making a landing when lightning struck a tree right next door on Gilligan's Island, splitting it cleanly down the middle with an ear-splitting crash. The electrical charge set the girls' hair on end. Elly tried not to panic, but she dropped the paddle and it sailed right by her outstretched hand. By now, the rain was coming down in torrents. Battered by the wind and waves, the little canoe was flooding rapidly.

"It's all right," Robin yelled over the storm. "We're almost there, hang on, Elly." The young girl fought against the conditions and shortly, the canoe's bow beached on the sand in the island's cove.

The girls jumped out and ran, it was uncannily dark despite short intervals of flashes. They could barely hear each other over the roar. Robin grabbed Cresselley's hand and charged down the barely visible path, dodging fallen tree limbs that strewed the narrow trail. Without warning, the little structure eerily appeared directly in front of the girls. Robin rapidly pulled back the canvas flap which functioned as a door and the two were met with bloodcurdling screams. Cresselley jumped back, but Robin, in the lead, could see two young girls huddled together in the back. She stepped in, pulling Cresselley behind her.

"It's all right, we're the Spenser twins. Did you get caught in the storm too?"

It was almost impossible for either party to hear the other clearly, but the two petrified children nodded.

"Our grandmother is going to be so mad at us," the younger of the two shouted over the roar of the storm.

"No, she won't," Cresselley reassured. "She'll be proud that you were smart and found shelter. You're Mrs. Chapman's granddaughters?"

The girls nodded but that was all the conversation possible. The thunder vibrated the shack and the wind caught the canvas flap, thrashing it with pounding force against the side of the enclosure.

Robin swiftly grabbed the securing twine and wrestled it tightly around a support beam. In the subsequent flashes, she could see the little girls were trembling under crushing fear.

She crawled next to Cresselley and spoke loudly in her ear, "Let's make a comfort circle."

Her sister nodded and the twins moved into position, encircling the younger girls, placing their arms around their small, quivering shoulders.

"Put your heads in the middle and look at the floor," Robin instructed.

When the girls complied, she began to sing, "Bees'll buzz, kids'll blow dandelion fuzz, and we'll all be doing whatever snow does—*in summer*..."

Cresselley smiled and joined in. To the twins' delight, their little companions did as well.

"A drink in my hand. My snow up against the burning sand. Prob'ly getting gorgeously tanned—*in summer*!"

The singers were unexpectedly interrupted by the crash of a tree branch coming down near their shelter, the top leaves brushing the roofline just above their heads.

"It'll pass," Robin reassured the little group. "Hang on, it won't be this bad much longer." She could see in the faint light the youngest was looking at her with gratitude.

"This has been one bizarre week at the lake," she noted.

"Other than a rogue thunderstorm before lunch?" Robin asked.

The little girl hesitated as another flash of lightening immediately followed by thunder temporarily disrupted her.

"Rach, wait until they can hear us better," her sister advised.

Eventually, the storm began to move off to the south. The lightning grew fainter, the rain let up some, and the sky showed some brightening on the northern horizon.

"We might get a rainbow out of this," Cresselley took an optimistic tone. "Let's venture outside, it should be safe now."

One by one, the girls exited their little sanctuary into the late morning. The air was noticeably cooler and less humid. It was still raining lightly, but the dense trees blocked the view of any rainbow that might be forming over the lake. Although the four of them were already dripping wet, the girls stepped back into the shelter out of what was left of the storm.

"We're so rude," the oldest of the little girls apologized, "I'm Britain, like the country, and this is Rachel. We're staying with our grandmother for two weeks while our parents are in Europe. I think our nana knows your gram. She works in the post office, right?"

"That's right." Cresselley smiled. "We're staying in her cottage on the other side of the lake for the summer. Tell us about the weird things this week?"

"You know Nana's house, big windows in the front, dormers on the roof, a real panoramic view. That's the word, right?"

Robin chuckled. "Good word, you can see a lot!"

"Well, we have a loft-type setup on the third floor, it's spectacular! The first night we couldn't sleep, so we were stargazing. Don't tell Nana, she doesn't know this part."

"Your secret is safe with us, we have a few of our own Grammy isn't aware of."

"So anyway, we're looking out and all of a sudden, these two dim lights, maybe flashlights or lanterns, are moving along on the side of the hill past the 'No Trespassing' sign," Britain explained.

"It was really creepy," Rachel added.

"They disappeared pretty fast, but we definitely saw them," Britain continued. "We watched for about a half an hour more and thought we saw a few flickers higher up the hill, that was it. Then the next day, we were helping Nana weed the flower garden and this big, black SUV went speeding past us to the end of the lane."

"Nana wasn't happy. Everyone who lives there is suspicious of cars they don't recognize, being a dead end and all," Rachel explained. "On top of that, it had tinted windows, so you couldn't see who was inside. Nana tried to walk up to the driver's side, but just as she got close, it spun around and went flying past us back down the dirt road."

"That's scary," Cresselley sympathized.

"It was to us," Britain agreed. "Nana was furious, she went in the house and phoned Officer Mendez's headquarters. He was out on a call somewhere, but he did come by later in the day. We were making strawberry jam, which you can't just put on pause, so Nana asked us to meet him at the door and show him the SUVs tracks. That gave us a chance to tell him about the lights on the hill in private. He promised not to tell our grandmother how late we were up that night."

"Brit, remember what he asked us," Rachael added.

"That's right, I forgot that part. Officer Mendez asked us if we'd noticed the license plate on the car. We told him we didn't see the numbers but that it was orangey."

"Like a New York plate," Robin suggested.

"Yes, exactly," Britain confirmed. "He told us that was very helpful."

Cresselley glanced over at Robin and as she expected, her sister was listening intently to the Chapman girls' disclosure.

"Let's see how the weather is doing," she suggested. "We need to get you girls home. Where did you park?"]

Britain and Rachael laughed at the vehicle reference.

"On the east cove side of the island," Britain explained. "We brought the rowboat."

"I'm pretty sure it's as swamped as our canoe," Robin presumed. "Elly, I'll go get our craft and meet you on the other side. Go with the girls and see if you can bail it out. Do you have anything secured in the boat to bail with?" she asked the pair.

"We have a sawed-off Clorox bottle tied to the seat, so it should still be there."

"Good for you, that's planning seamanship style," Cresselley complimented.

The two beamed at the acknowledgment. The girls parted in opposite directions toward their pre-assigned tasks. It wasn't difficult for Robin to roll the canoe on its side and watch the water run out while rescuing the blueberries floating in their bowls. She glanced around briefly to see if Elly's missing paddle had washed ashore on the island, but it was nowhere to be seen. Undeterred, Robin put on her life jacket and jumped in. When she reached the east cove end of the island, the trio was making progress, but the rowboat was still almost completely submerged and the young Chapman girls looked discouraged, exhausted.

"Brit, Rach, take a break, you've been through enough this morning. Don't worry, Elly and I've had plenty of teamwork practice. Bye. Bye, blueberries, you're bird feed now," she tweaked while emptying the containers.

Bailing with ferocity, a bowl in each hand, as her twin manned the Clorox bottle, the rowboat was soon floating as though it had never rained.

"How did you two ever manage to row this monster?" Elly laughed.

"We sat side by side on the seat and each had an oar," Britain explained.

"Are you sure you're not twins?" Robin teased. "That takes an incredible amount of coordination."

The girls smiled from their perch with appreciation.

"Okay, here's the plan, El, you want to row or paddle?"

"I'll row," Cresselley chose wisely. "Dad gives my jay stroke a D."

"Okay, Huck and Tom, you heard the captain, life jackets and boarding passes. Next stop, Chapman's Landing."

The young sisters were visibly relieved that there would be no more rowing in their immediate future. They gladly donned their flotation devices and joined Captain Cresselley for the voyage home, even as they dreaded their grandmother's disapproval.

"We are going to be so grounded," Rachael voiced what they both were thinking. "The rule is, check the weather report before going anywhere near the water."

"We're in the same boat," Cresselley admitted. "That's our rule too, and guess what, we didn't check either. Don't worry, we'll back you up."

As the little rowboat rounded the point and the Chapman dock came into view, the figure of an anxious grandmother was unmistakable. Binoculars in hand, the girls could see her waving frantically with unambiguous relief as she spotted the little armada. Robin quickly passed the rowboat and reached the dock just ahead of Cresselley and her precious cargo.

"Nana," the girls shouted. "We're so sorry, we promise to follow the rules from now on."

Before Robin could convince Mrs. Chapman that the girls were safe, the seventy-five-year-old matriarch slid off the end of the dock, waist-high in water, arms outstretched. "Don't you ever scare me like that again," but it was far from scolding.

The girls' Nana couldn't wait to squeeze them, so she did just that, tilting over the side of the boat, tears streaming down her face. Finally satisfied they were unharmed, she turned her attention to the twins. "I can't thank you dears enough for brining my darlings safely home from the grips of that terrible storm. How on earth did you manage? I was sure that big maple next to the house was going to take out the roof."

"Your granddaughters got to the shelter on Boy Scout Island before we did," Robin explained. "They were very resourceful, and brave!"

Britain and Racheal smiled graciously, but they weren't inclined to take credit for being anything but petrified.

"Elly and Robin saved us," they proclaimed emphatically. "We were so scared, Nana."

"Well, I can't wait to tell your grandmother how heroic you twins were in such a perilous situation."

"Please don't tell her," Elly implored. "It would be better if she doesn't know. We don't want her worrying endlessly about what we're doing when she's working."

"I see your point, sweetheart. Mum's the word. Won't you come in and dry off? I can make some hot cocoa."

"We need to get home, but we'd like to ask a favor if we could."

"Anything," Mrs. Chapman offered.

"Would you call Carol? She's probably pacing our dock right about now," Robin speculated.

"Absolutely, anything else I can do for my granddaughters' new best friends?"

"I dropped my canoe paddle," Elly confessed. "Maybe you have one I could borrow for the trip home?"

"I'll get one," Rachael jumped at the chance to be reciprocal, dashing off toward the boathouse.

The girls promised to stay in touch, waving as the canoe and its occupants headed back toward open water.

"I hope the reception we get is just as forgiving," Cresselley confessed softly.

Robin didn't reply but thought warmly about her time with Carol on the dock that morning.

The girls were just passing Blueberry Island when the sound of an outboard motor reached them. As the craft came into view, Robin groaned.

"Sweet indictments, here we go. That's the Lake Association President, coming to charge us with reckless seamanship."

"Be fair, Robbie. There may have been others on the water and he's just concerned."

"Hey, young ladies, enjoying the weather?" the driver shouted, bringing the versatile Bayliner alongside at an idle.

"It's lovely," Robin didn't mask her sarcasm.

"Well, your water taxi is here," he announced. "Cresselley, looks like you're first up the ladder."

"We're fine," Robin objected. "We can finish paddling home."

"No can do, girls."

"Carol called you," Robin assumed.

"Not just Carol," John Weissmuller informed, "Mrs. Chapman as well. Sorry, ladies, I don't want to get into trouble with two 'momma bears.' Up you go, bowman."

Cresselley was relieved that Robin stopped protesting, she was soaking wet and the rowboat had taken its toll on her back. She was sore and worn-out. Mr. Weissmuller gently draped a towel over Cresselley's shoulders as she climbed over the stern. Surrendering, Robin tossed the canoe's bowline to him and dutifully followed her sister aboard. The outboard chugged along at a modest eight miles per hour, pulling the canoe at a safe distance behind. No one spoke until Robin surprised Cresselley with a line of questions for the Lake Association President.

"Do you know any details about the Barkers' house fire?" she directed her question at the helmsman.

"Not much," he responded. "I got a call at our main residence in Trumbull from an FBI detective back in April. He didn't offer any details about the fire, just a curtesy call informing me for the association members that the boat launch would be closed for an unspecified amount of time. I expressed my surprise at the timing. It was just before opening day of fishing season and there would be a lot of disappointed sportsmen. He cited the need for an investigation and abruptly hung up."

"Is the investigation closed?" Robin redirected.

"I have no idea," the president admitted. "I never heard from him or anyone else after that. I did stop in to see Officer Mendez a few weeks ago when we were here opening the lake house."

"What did he say?" Robin's attitude had changed to respectful curiosity.

"He was uncharacteristically vague," Mr. Weissmuller acknowledged. "I had a feeling he knew more than he was authorized to share. He did suggest a cautionary note to our members about staying clear of off-trail outings around the lake until further notice. I must admit, I didn't give it more thought after the boat launch reopened—that is, until now, Miss Spenser!"

As the girls predicted, Carol was waiting anxiously on the dock when the Bayliner pulled alongside.

"Thank you, John," she said sincerely as the girls climbed out and gave her a hug. "You poor things, you're soaked. Go change and I'll make you something warm for lunch. I'll be in after I chat with your maritime Uber driver."

The twins made no objection. Upstairs, Robin changed quickly and then lay on Cresselley's bed with her face against the window screen.

"What do you suppose they're talking about?" she commented, suspiciously observing the two adults on the dock.

"I don't know, the weather? What difference does it make, Miss Paranoia?"

"I doubt the association president told us everything he knows about what's going on around the lake. It's his business to know."

"Maybe, he thinks it's better for us if we don't know. We are twelve years old after all."

Robin didn't have a smart remark for her sister, but she was still stewing about it when the two joined Carol making soup in the kitchen.

"What were you and Mr. Weissmuller talking about after we left?" she interrogated.

"Storm damage," Carol was clearly surprised at Robin's tone. "Apparently there were three suspected tornado touch downs not far from town. He lost a big oak in his yard and it took out one side of a tool shed. Oh, and he warned me to keep you girls from going unaccompanied into the woods."

"What did you tell him?" Robin kept up her line of questioning.

Carol grinned. "I informed him that you stick to the road on your outings. You do, don't you?"

Robin relaxed. "Since the day we met Jesse," she reported truthfully. "Sorry, Carol, that wasn't fair. The soup smells awesome."

"You can thank the Campbell's."

"Carol, can we go to the Stillman Road house this afternoon. I need to do some laundry."

"Sure thing. How about you, Robbie, laundry?"

"I could do a load." Robin grinned. Her doing laundry was about as rare as Carol making lunch.

"Tonight, I am taking you ladies to Louis's restaurant for dinner." Carol's boyfriend was co-owner and one of the chefs at a new seafood restaurant in the borough. "Why don't you invite Jesse to come with us?"

"Oh, that would be so cool!" Cresselley clamored. "We'll text him right now and try to call him later from the landline at the house for details. What's the name of the restaurant?"

"Carpathia's Catch," Carol answered.

"Wait a second," Robin interjected, "isn't that the ship that res-cued what was left of Titanic's passengers in lifeboats?"

"That's the one. She made sad but vital catches, didn't she? One of them was Louis's partner's great-great-grandmother. She boarded Titanic at Cherbourg. The front of the menu tells her story."

The girls were speechless. They loaded their laundry hampers in the car and waited for Carol to join them.

"Did you manage to contact Jesse?" she asked sliding into the driver's seat.

"We did," Cresselley answered enthusiastically. "He and his Dad left work early because of power outages from the storm. We'll call him about a pick-up time from the house, he's home."

"How about six o'clock. I'm going to have Louis make us special reservations by the big front windows. It looks over the harbor with all the moored and docked fishing boats. You two could use a little tranquility after the morning you spent."

Already, the Stillman Road house smelled as though no one was living there, a faint musty odor met the girls when they unlocked the door.

"Let's turn on the dehumidifier," Carol suggested, "and see what the basement is like. We might need to visit a little more often."

"I'll come with," Cresselley followed Carol downstairs. "I want to get some chicken out of the freezer and start the first load of clothes."

Robin picked up the landline and called Jesse. Before she could even say "Hello," he was urgently whispering over the line. "Cresselley, is that you? We need time to talk without adult ears around tonight. I have an incredible story to tell you two about…you know."

"Jessie, it's Robbie, but I got all that."

"Oh, hey, Robbie. You'll never guess, I found out where the FBI agent is staying—right here in town. Can't wait to tell you what happened yesterday, but I gotta go. Acey needs to go out."

"See you at six." Robin ended the call.

Dinner in the Borough

When the girls picked Jesse up early that evening, he was impeccably attired.

"Don't you look nice," Carol complimented.

"My mom picked my clothes," Jesse admitted. "I'm not much of a dresser."

"Neither am I," Robin sympathized. Carol had insisted she wear a sundress and the young girl looked particularly uncomfortable in it.

Louis met them at the door and escorted the party of four to the best table in the restaurant just as Carol had promised. Introductions were made and Louis signaled their waiter, retreating to his work in the kitchen.

"I'll catch up to you at break." He smiled at Carol.

"How about we share an order of steamers for an appetizer?" she suggested. "Do you like clams, Jesse?"

"I'm a fan of all seafood except maybe calamari."

"Good." Carol gave the initial order to the waiter as the youngsters poured over the menu. "I'm going with Block Island swordfish," she announced.

Robin and Jesse picked fish and chips, Cresselley decided after great lengths on broiled scallops.

"Sometimes, Dad's perception of guilt about not being home enough has a fine benefit"—Robin gave Carol a perceptive glance—"We'd rather live in a tent and have him with us, but if he's not here and wants to buy us dinner, we're not above taking advantage of his generosity."

Louis appeared just as everyone was finishing. "Do you mind if I steal Carol for about twenty minutes?" He smiled. "I'm sending over something to keep you busy."

"We'll be fine, this place is awesome," Jesse observed. "I could spend hours looking at the history in pictures on the walls."

"Check out the men's room," Louis suggested. "There are more prints of Titanic's kitchen and first-class dining area." He smiled and led Carol out to the deck.

The minute they were out of earshot, Jesse leaned into the table and spoke with unexpected urgency.

"I need to talk fast," he cautioned. "So much happened yesterday, I still can't believe it. My dad and I are rewiring a barn on Hangman Hill," Jesse began, "and the owner wants special battery-operated outdoor floodlights for power outages. When we pulled up at Drew's hardware store in the village, the car that FBI agent was driving when he came to the house was parked in front and sure enough, here he comes out the door with a big box. Dad didn't notice, he was busy looking for a parking spot. You know Drew's, nobody can find anything in that store, and I think he likes it that way. When Dad asked about the lights, he says his last customer just bought the three he had in stock. I'm thinking, why would the FBI dude want something like that unless he's up to surveillance off the grid? They have motion detectors, great at night which seems to be when these suspects are active. I really want to drill Drew for info, so I ask to use the men's room. Dad cooperates, says he'll order the units and meet me in the truck. He's gone when I get back to the counter and man, does Drew spill. He doesn't know the customer's name, he always pays in cash, but he's pretty sure the man is renting one of the cabins at the rotary since he's always commenting on the state of the place. This is great info, and I'm about to leave, but he goes on—tells me every time the buyer comes in, he has questions about stuff in town. Remember when Bess Eaton closed, and the historic, old Duffer Men's Club was out of a coffee spot for their early morning gossip?"

The girls nodded.

"Well, Drew set up a self-serve counter and tables for them in the front window and they gladly relocated. I didn't even ask Drew to include them in the conversation, he went right to it, bellowing across the room, 'Hey, Ansel, what was that last guy in here asking you about the other day?'"

"The Crossroads." Robin gasped and looked at Cresselley, but Jesse didn't notice.

"Well, tell this nice kid about it," Jesse mimicked Drew's drawl.

"He wanted to know the history of the place," Ansel reported.

"What did you tell him?"

"I told him it's all crumbling and overgrown now, but it was a heck of a watering hole until the last of the mills closed in the thirties." Jesse paused his account long enough to glance over his shoulder to make sure Carol was still on the deck and let his companions absorb his happenstances.

"Jesse, you are one clever investigator!" Cresselley complimented.

"Must be the mystery novels," the young man blushed. "Let me finish while I've got the chance."

But before Jesse could continue, their waiter appeared carrying a bulky tray. He stepped up to the table and set a massive strawberry shortcake in front of each of them.

"This is going to be a challenge even for me." Jesse thanked the waiter.

"Thank Louis"—the waiter smiled—"this is his specialty."

Once he retreated to the kitchen, Jesse resumed.

"Those cabins Drew mentioned are on the way to Hangman Hill, so when we drove by, I looked for the car. It was parked in front of unit three."

"This is phenomenal," Robin avowed with excitement. "We can approach that FBI agent now."

"But how?" Cresselley wondered. "We can't exactly ask Carol to drop us off there for an hour or so."

"You're right," Jesse agreed. "My dad would interrogate me if I ever suggested a visit and it's too far for us to get there by ourselves, even on bikes. Besides, we wouldn't know if he was around until we saw the car or an empty parking spot."

"And what would we say to him other than speculation?" Cresselley added. "We still don't have any concrete evidence."

The table grew quiet.

"You made some incredible discoveries yesterday, Jesse, wait till you hear about our morning," Robin broke the silence, but the discussion ended abruptly when Louis's voice called them back to reality.

"How is everyone doing?" he inquired politely.

"We need doggie bags for this perfect creation," Cresselley lightened the mood among the diners.

"Even you, Jesse?" Louis teased.

"Hey, I'm not giving up yet," Jesse proclaimed with a big grin

"Thanks for lending me, Carol, I need to get back to the kitchen before my partner reports me missing." He squeezed Carol's hand and acknowledged the "thumbs up" from the dinner guests.

Carol headed off to the ladies' room, leaving the little group alone, when suddenly a bartender approached and handed Jesse a piece of folded paper.

"What's this?" Jesse looked up puzzled.

"A man at the bar asked me to deliver it to you, he just left."

Jesse didn't pause to ask questions, but quickly strode to a window overlooking the parking lot. A black SUV with tinted windows and New York license plates was speeding through the lot, passing just below. The numbers were a blur to Jesse as he watched the vehicle head south on the Borough's narrow exit road. Looking disappointed, he rejoined the girls with a description.

"That's the car Britain and Rachael saw." Cresselley gulped.

"Who?" Jesse appeared bewildered but before the girls could explain their day, Carol returned and the four left the restaurant together.

"You're all uncommonly quiet," Carol commented as she turned the little Prius back onto Route #1 heading home. "Do you want the radio or a playlist?"

"Not necessary," Robin answered, adding, "Louis is really cool, Carol."

"His parents brought him here from Peru when he was two."

Robin didn't feel much like small talk, but it was imperative the three didn't raise her suspicions.

"Is that who inspired him to cook?" Cresselley took over.

"Actually, it was his grandmother. His parents worked long hours to support the family." Carol sensibly reached over and turned the radio on.

Robin pulled a napkin with the restaurant's log from her dress pocket and began to write.

Looking over her shoulder Jesse read, "What note say?" He took the pencil and the napkin, "No chance," he scribbled then pulled the folded paper from his pocket.

Together they read, "*Children shouldn't play adult games. They might get hurt.*"

Robin reclaimed the napkin. "Asked BT for description."

Jesse looked at Robin with admiration.

"What did the bartender say?" he whispered.

"Tall, brown hair, distinctive tattoo on inner arm."

Cresselley again distracted Carol with comments on dinner, so the other two could finished their conversation.

"What do you mean distinctive?" Jesse whispered.

"Lion's head," Robin spoke softly. "Can you make copies of the note?"

"On Dad's printer."

"Good, I'll mail one to the FBI agent as soon as possible."

"I can drop them in your paper box tomorrow morning about seven o'clock when my dad and I drive by, but we don't know his name. I can look for the report he left on the fire, but that's risky."

"No problem, I'll address it care of Cady's Cabins, occupant unit three, and add my cell number."

"Smart! What's this about two other girls seeing the car I described?"

"Long story, but it was suspiciously at the end of Murray Road a few days ago." Robin quickly filled Jesse in on the events of the morning, the storm, and what the Chapman sisters had told them.

She had just about finished when Carol pulled into the Bostick's driveway.

"Mom wants to have a picnic lunch for you after the fourth of July," Jesse announced. "I think she's worried I'm taking advantage of your hospitality."

"Well, tell her we are taking advantage of your company." Carol chuckled. "And we would be delighted to come, wouldn't we, girls?

"Absolutely," the twins chimed.

A Clue in the Note

Cresselley woke early with a start, having experienced a nightmare so vivid it still seemed real in the morning light. Someone was chasing her through the woods. As the footsteps closed in on her, she came to a clearing with a cemetery she didn't recognize. Right in the middle, there was a large headstone big enough for her to crouch behind and hide. As she ran toward it, the engraved name and dates became clear—it was her mother's. Feeling protected, she darted behind the stone as the footsteps came closer. Glancing sideways, she noted the adjacent grave marker, it read "Robert Shawn Spenser." She gasped and woke up before she could read the dates. Shaken, Cresselley sat up in bed fighting the urge to wake Robin, but the dream would either make her laugh or upset her too.

The clock on the wall read 6:45. What time did Jesse say he'd drop off the copies? She was reasonably sure he had said seven o'clock. The twin went to the closet and took out some clothes. She'd get dressed and head out to the paper box. There was something nagging about that note. Not what it threatened, but the handwriting. She wanted time to have a detailed look at it before Robin got up.

Jesse was as good as his word. The copies, along with the original, were already in the box when Cresselley looked a few minutes after seven o'clock. She dropped the morning paper on the table and went quietly back to her room. There was a "Post-it" attached to the envelope. "Talk at 5:00," it read. The twin only had a few minutes to examine the note before she heard Robbie's feet hit the floor in the other room, quickly followed by her disheveled, groggy sister standing in the door.

"Are those from Jesse?" she asked, rubbing her eyes. "Doing a little investigative work this early?"

"Robbie, sit." Cresselley patted the edge of the bed. "Take a look at this."

Robin yawned and obeyed.

"See this print?"

"Looks intentionally blunt," Robin observed.

"Exactly but look closely at the *h*'s here in 'children' and again in 'shouldn't' and 'they.' Whose writing does that look like?"

"It looks like cursive, how Gram writes."

"And Mom's, feminine. Also, the words children, play. If a man wrote that, wouldn't it be delinquents or juveniles even?"

"So you think the ringleader is a woman?"

"I do. But she's not camping out in the cave or hiking the woods at night, she's pulling the strings on multiple puppets."

"Like the dude from the bar who sent this note last night."

"Exactly, and torched the Barkers' house, drove the SUV the Chapman girls saw, and parked by the cemetery the night Jesse and his dad went by."

"There's something else bugging me," Robin acknowledged. "How did they know we were getting close to their little operation and follow us to the restaurant?"

Cresselley was pensive for a minute then looked at Robin.

"Remember the first morning we met Jesse and then went on to the cave?"

"Sure."

"We were singing and talking pretty loudly. What if they heard us and were nearby, watching where we went?"

"You were jumpy at the cave. Did you see anything?"

"No, but I had an eerie feeling of eyes on us."

"And they probably saw Jesse talking to us that morning and maybe even the next day at lunch."

"But why threaten us? We've never actually seen them. The only thing we have is a vague description and a lion's head tattoo. Why not just move their operation somewhere else?"

"I wondered that too," Robin agreed. "Just suppose they're running drugs. There might be a shipment in the pipeline that can't be intercepted. They'd be forced to see it through before the move."

"Makes sense," Cresselley approved. "Oh, Robbie, there was a Post-it attached to the copies." She handed her sister the note.

"It sounds urgent, hope nothing has happened."

The girls were interrupted by Carol.

"Hey, ladies," she called from the foot of the stairs. "What time do you expect your grandmother for dinner tonight?"

"About six," Robin speculated.

"I don't like leaving early, but I'm meeting Louis's parents and it's about an hour drive."

"No worries, we'll be fine. We have prep work to do in the kitchen.

"Can we go to the village for fresh veggies before you leave?" Cresselley was thinking ahead.

"Sure, right after you girls have breakfast."

Robin glance over at Cresselley and noted, "This is good actually. We can talk to Jesse in complete privacy when he calls at five o'clock. Hey, do you remember the street number of Cady's Cabins? I want to get the copy of our unexpected correspondence in the mailbox before the delivery comes around noon."

"Pretty sure it's 389. I only noticed because the Darien house was 289."

"This could be a long afternoon waiting to talk to Jesse," Robin observed. "Wait, I have an idea. Let's return the canoe paddle to the Chapman girls and find out if they've noticed anything else peculiar going on."

"That's a tremendous idea, a follow-up inquiry. Hope their parents are still enjoying Europe."

Return to the North Cove

Britain and Rachael were busy raking their grandmother's beach when the twins paddled around the point and entered the north cove. They jumped up and down waving when they spotted the canoe.

"Elly, Robbie, I was going to text you," Britain shouted. "We have news."

Once the craft was beached and the borrowed paddle stored in the boathouse, the four retreated to lawn chairs on the dock.

"We saw the black SUV with tinted windows and the orangey license plate again," Rachael began.

"It was hidden at the top of Cassidy Hill," Britain continued. "You know, that long, straight stretch with no houses."

"Hidden?" Cresselley questioned. "You mean like off the road?"

"Not just off the road, covered up with branches. We were on our way with Nana to pick blueberries at Maple Acres. It wouldn't have looked as suspicious if we hadn't recognized it, and then it was gone when we came back."

"That is shadowy," Cresselley agreed. "I wonder what they were doing in that part of town. It's nowhere near the bear cave or here."

"Well, actually it is," Robin almost whispered.

She had the girls' attention; they leaned in with expectant faces.

"Dad's map on the wall in my room."

Cresselley nodded in acknowledgment.

"If you look at it closely, the state forest to the west of the cave and northeast of the boat launch goes all the way through to Cassidy Hill. It's several miles by car, but as the crow flies, maybe a few hours hike, depending on the overgrowth."

"Do you think they were rendezvousing with someone or something?" Cresselley was aware of the way her sister's mind put things together.

"I'm not sure, but geographically, all of these places are connected and secluded, like the bear cave and your family cemetery, Brit and Rach."

Rachael beamed. "I'm named after a great-great-aunt buried there."

"You girls are naturals at surveillance. When are your parents coming home?"

"Sadly, tomorrow. Not that we aren't eager to see them," Rachael quickly added. "We'll spend the Fourth of July with Mom's relatives, they're great but no lake."

"We'll be back almost every weekend for the rest of summer vacation though." Britain smiled.

"So we'll get to see more of you!" Cresselley declared. "Give our best to your nana."

As their grandmother's dock came into view, Cresselley in the bow turned to Robin. "Look what's tied up."

Robin swung the stern to get a clear view. "Blue Girl is back for the season. We can go knee boarding when Dad gets home. Carol's father must have finished with the new seats and put it in at the boat launch! How great is that."

"We probably missed him. Carol needs to leave soon. She must have given her dad a ride back to his truck and boat trailer. We'll have to thank him later."

Carol was eager to depart when the girls beached the canoe. She waved goodbye and climbed into the Prius. Robin lit the grill for dinner and the twins relaxed on the dock, awaiting five o'clock.

Just as promised, Robin's phone buzzed precisely at the hour.

"Jesse, you're on speaker, is everything okay?"

"Hey, Robbie, Elly, I've got some bad news."

"What's happened?" Cresselley asked anxiously.

"My dad and I have a road job, we're leaving late tonight for Quincey, Mass. It's just outside of Boston."

"For how long?" Robin asked. "Not the rest of the summer, I hope."

"Probably four or five days. I wish I didn't have to go but the money is good and they put us up in a classy hotel."

"Five days, that's not too bad, we'll miss you though," Cresselley observed with sincerity.

"I know, but I'll worry the whole time about what the two of you are up to. Did you get the copies?"

"We did and put one in the mail already. Don't worry, this is all in the FBI guys hands once he gets it. We'll tell him what we know and leave it at that."

Why am I doubtful?" Jesse laughed. "But I'm serious, you two, no cave explorations, no graveyard picnics, and no excursions in thunderstorms, promise me."

"We promise," Cresselley assured.

"Robin?" Jesse insisted.

"Look who's gone all adult on us," Robin taunted. "Fine, I promise too."

"Girls," Jesse paused. There was a long silence as the twins waited for him to continue. "Go to the library!"

They laughed at the recommendation. "Get back soon!"

"I will, say hi to Carol," Jesse added and hung up.

The girls looked at each other with disappointment.

"Five days isn't that long," Robin tried to be optimistic.

Cresselley sighed. "Let's finish getting dinner ready and remember, Robbie, light conversation tonight."

The girls were setting the table when the screen door got their attention.

Grammy Tells a Story

"Grammy, you're here!"

"There are my beautiful girls." Grandma Spenser embraced the twins lovingly. "How was your first week of summer vacation in the cottage? You're both so thin. Is Carol feeding you well?"

"She isn't the cook you are, Grammy, but she does her best. Besides, we can cook for ourselves. Wait until you see what we've put together for dinner."

"That's wonderful, girls. There isn't much ready in the garden yet, but I brought you some red leaf lettuce and a few radishes."

"Thanks, Gram, we love everything you grow. Carol took us to Ed's farm stand this morning and we got some early corn. A salad will go great with what we've concocted." Robin was the lesser of the two kitchen enthusiasts, but she did usually do the bulk of the dishes.

"What is Carol doing on her first night off?"

"She's going to meet her boyfriend's parents and had to leave a little early."

The girls expected their grandmother would not be especially concerned about the time they spent unsupervised but were still hopeful Mrs. Chapman had kept her word about their escapade in the storm.

"Gram, we set the table on the porch so you can go sit down, we'll get to serving. Is Italian dressing okay?" Elly genuinely liked the role of hostess.

"Oh, yes, honey, Italian is perfect. Wow, Carol's dad finished your father's boat," she observed stepping onto the porch. "I've always admired Arthur. He could fix anything from the time he was a young boy."

"He sure works miracles with Blue Girl's age-related ailments." Cresselley laughed. "Robbie, if it's ready, can you bring in the 'piece de resistance'?" Cresselley was anxious to impress their grandmother.

"Are you girls taking up French cooking? I recall how much you loved the film with Meryl Streep about Julia Childs."

"Dinner is about as all American as you can get," Robin gave her grandmother a hint.

"Oh, and the corn is such a treat. I must admit I'm envious of Ed's greenhouses, and he has tomatoes already?"

Robin appeared at the porch screen door with a platter in her hand. "Look, Gram, we barbecued chicken! Dad is the real grill master, but we've watched him enough times to attempt it by ourselves."

"Oh, you girls are just growing up way too fast for your old grandmother."

"You're not old, Grammy," Elly reassured her. "You still work in the post office five days a week."

"Gram, how are the Barkers?" Robin changed the topic.

"Oh, they're fine, girls. They went to Texas back in November and their mail hasn't been routed back through our post office yet. Do you remember their oldest son, Roy?"

"Oh yes," Cresselley replied. "He took us for a sail with Mom on his Hobie Cat."

"I'd forgotten about that pretty catamaran," their grandmother admitted. "Well, he and his wife had the Barkers' first grandchild, they went to visit and haven't yet returned. Can't say that I blame them, I know how wonderful it is to be near your grandchildren."

"We sure have missed Dad since our move, but now we get to see you all the time, Gram," Robin agreed. "Well, I don't know about you two, but I'm diving into this chicken, I'm ravenous." Honoring her promise to her sister for light conversation, Robin addressed her grandmother. "Grammy, there is something we've wanted to ask you about for a while now. You might not know the answer, but Dad doesn't seem to want to discuss anything that happened when Mom was alive."

"Yes, dear, ask away. If there is anything I can help you with, you know I will."

"Where do our names come from?" Elly jumped in knowing exactly where her sister was going with her inquiry.

"Your names"—their grandmother chuckled—"Your parents never told you?"

"Did Dad really want a boy to be named after him and that's how I got to be Robin?"

"No, no, sweetie," Grandmother was emphatic, "your parents just wanted you to be healthy. Of course, in the beginning, they were only expecting one, so they decided your mother would name the baby regardless of the sex."

"When did they find out we were twins?" Robin wanted to know.

"At the first ultrasound, I think it was about seven weeks into the pregnancy."

"Were they overwhelmed?" It was Elly's turn to question.

"They were thrilled, they phoned me at the post office from the doctor's office. It was such an unexpected gift, each of them would name one of you."

"Which one of them named me?" Elly asked. "Was it Mom?"

"Well, girls, they flipped a coin to determine which one of them would name the firstborn."

"So whoever won that coin toss named me," Robin stated with confidence, "I'm the oldest by five minutes. Mom told us that much at our fifth birthday party."

"That's right, honey, your dad won with heads."

"So Mom named me then," Elly surmised. "But where did she ever come up with Cresselley? Who's heard of anyone named that. Most of my teachers can't even pronounce it."

"Well, that's actually a beautiful story just like you, sweetheart."

"Tell us, Grammy, we love your stories," Robin was just as curious as her twin about the origins of the name.

"I don't know how much information you've been given about your mother's side of the family," Grandmother began. "You know your grandparents were killed in a car accident before your parents were even married."

"Did they meet Dad before that happened?" asked Robin.

"Oh yes. I even met them once when your parents were dating as seniors in high school. They moved to Denver right after the children graduated and went on to college, so I never saw them again. But to get to the story, we need to go back another generation, to your maternal great-grandmother. Her maiden name was Griffiths and her family lived in Wales until she was twelve, just like you girls, when her father moved the family to America. They lived in a beautiful area of Wales called Pembrokeshire, and it was home to a large estate owned for many, many generations by the Allen family. Can you guess the name of the estate?"

"I'm named after a house?" Cresselley was indignant.

"Not just a house, honey, an attractive mansion and all of the grounds. The Allen family was beloved by the townspeople and still is today. The village hunt on horseback has been sponsored by the estate for two hundred years. So your mother, having heard all these stories, wanted to honor her grandmother's heritage and quite frankly, sweetie, I think your name is unique and lovely."

"Well, I'm beginning to think so too," Cresselley admitted. "From what you are telling us, Grammy, it's still there."

"Oh yes, girls. I think the Allen family is on its eighth generation with an heir apparent interested in keeping the lineage. But like so many of the big estates in the United Kingdom, the family has had to be creative to pay the taxes and the upkeep. If I am not mistaken, you can rent rooms by the night there now, just like a hotel. That whole area is an attractive tourist destination. So you see, my dear, you are the namesake for an elegant old girl who is expensive to keep in 'paint and powder,' so to speak."

"That's what Daddy says about the sailboat Grandpa built," Robin jumped in.

"How remarkable that you bring up a nautical reference," the girls' grandmother whispered, "the Allen's made a great deal of money through a lighthouse."

"A lighthouse, how does a lighthouse make a lot of money?" the girls were absolutely intrigued.

The family owned some waterfront property about twenty-five miles from what became their estate. It overlooked a treacherous sea-lane leading into an important port. I think it was in the early 1700s, the Allen patriarch at the time lobbied for a lighthouse lease, which would make the passage safer for the vessels that sailed through. It was a welcomed enterprise for the ships' captains and their owners, despite the fee, much like a toll, that was charged for each voyage that benefitted from the lighthouse. It was very lucrative for the Allen family until the end of the lease, ninety-nine years later. Of course, there were also marriages with heiresses to help with the family coffers and the rent on farmland."

"Grammy," Elly hated to interrupt the story, "how on earth do you know all of this?"

"Your mother told me a great deal of it when I stayed with her right after the two of you were born. Your father was busy with a big case at the time, and I was so happy to be able to help and be with you. Oh, and of course…I Googled it."

The girls laughed so hard, Robin almost tumbled off her footstool. When she regained her composure, she addressed her grandmother. "Grammy, you fox! We had no idea you knew how to do any of that, never mind, an interest."

"Well, I guess this old fox can still learn a few new tricks!"

"Gram, did you find the information about renting rooms there on the internet?"

"Yes, dear, I did."

"Oh, Grammy," Cresselley implored, "we must go before we graduate and head off to college."

"You girls won't get any argument from me," their grandmother assured, "I can't make promises, but perhaps we could go during your February vacation from school. The post office isn't particularly busy that time of year and from what I looked at online, there are some good deals for tourists in Wales during the off-peak season."

"Oh, Gram"—the twins threw their arms around her—"you're the best!"

"Robbie, I'm sorry I don't have a better answer concerning your name. You'll have to ask your father that one."

"It's okay, Gram. I'm probably named after Christopher Robin."

"Well, I did read him 'Winnie the Pooh.' But, honey, if it's any consolation, your middle name is my middle name and that was also your dad's choice."

"Thanks, Gram, I totally forgot about that. Actually, I'm okay with Robin."

The sound of a car in the driveway surprised the little group.

"Oh my"—Grandmother glanced at the clock over the fireplace—"look at the time. You ladies need your sleep."

"Before you go, Gram, just one more question, pleeeze," Robin begged.

"This one needs to be a quick one, girls."

"Is there a place called 'the Crossroads' near here?"

"The Crossroads," their grandmother frowned, "where did you hear about that?"

"Dad promised to take us exploring there when he's home one weekend before the end of summer," Robin explained.

"I haven't thought about that place in years. I would be surprised if your father can find it again. It must be all overgrown by now. I don't want you girls going into the woods by yourselves, you understand, don't you?" their grandmother's words had taken on a parental tone.

"Yes, Grammy," both agreed, but the look Robin shot her twin said volumes.

"Give your grandmother a big hug and I'll be off. Stop by the post office when you go to the library."

"Count on it," the girls echoed walking their grandmother to the door and saying good night to Carol.

At the top of the stairs where one twin went left and the other right, Robin whispered to her sister, "I knew it! This secretive place is somewhere around the lake, and I bet you it has a connection to whatever nefarious activities we stumbled on at the bear cave, and I know just how to get to the bottom of it."

"You are seriously going to get us put under house arrest or worse." Cresselley sighed. "And besides, we promised Jesse. Go to sleep and give that overactive imagination of yours a rest."

"But you haven't even heard my plan yet!"

"And I don't need to. GOOD NIGHT!" With that, Cresselley closed the bedroom door in her sister's face.

If the younger twin entertained any thought that her sister would let the mystery lie until Jesse returned, she was sadly disappointed at breakfast the next morning.

"Did you see the moon last night?" Robin asked of her as Elly sprinkled confectionary sugar over strawberry topped pancakes.

"Are you going to finish the dishes from last night or ask me stupid questions, girl? The only thing I saw after you finally let me go to bed was the inside of my eyelids."

"Well, it's a thin crescent, perfect for our spying mission, but we have to go tonight. I'm figuring about midnight."

"And just where do you propose we go at midnight?"

"It's pretty clear that most of this suspicious activity takes place in the cover of darkness. If we climb the fire tower, we can spot moving lights and see where they go."

"The bear cave and the cemetery must be at least a half mile from the fire tower. We won't be able to see much."

"I know, I already thought of that."

"Of course, you did." Elly rolled her eyes.

"Remember when we were little and Grammy rented the cottage every month of September to those bird-watchers?"

"You mean the old couple that moved to Florida? I think their name was Walden or maybe Waldo?"

"That's it! Sometimes, Elly, your memory is better than mine. I bet if we look in the storage space under the eaves, we'll find some of their stuff. They always left things behind and then he couldn't drive anymore, so they stopped coming."

"And that helps us see at night, how?"

"Binoculars, smarty. All bird-watchers have fantastic binoculars."

"Okay, I get your point. But why would I even consider leaving my comfortable bed to risk my life climbing nine flights of stairs in the dark to look for moving lights?"

"Because, sis, deep down you're just as curious as I am. And on top of that, I haven't complained about eating all this healthy stuff you've been creating. Confectionary sugar! What's wrong with maple syrup?"

"Your sugar highs get us into trouble," Elly responded. "Is Carol up yet? This is ready."

"Haven't seen her, want me to knock on her door?"

"No. but let's eat. I'll put some pancakes on warm in the oven for her."

The girls finished breakfast and headed for their hammocks on the lawn, each with a book under their arm. If this was going to be a long night, they would be wise to lay low all day. The twins had been reading for about forty-five minutes when a disheveled-looking Carol appeared on the porch.

"Okay, you imposters, who are you and what have you done with my two charges?" The girls giggled more at the sight Carol presented with her gnarly hairdo and bathrobe, a half-eaten pancake in hand, than her humor.

"Robbie, is that an actual book you have your nose so deeply buried in?"

Robin barely glanced back up at the mention of her name. Cresselley put her finger to her lips and winked at Carol, she was just as surprised with her sister's sudden, unexpected interest in the written word. In truth, no one was more credulous than Robin herself. She had discovered the paperback among Grammy's treasures in the bookcase above the fireplace. She wasn't sure which aspect of it she was most intrigued by, the title, *Mystery of the Mooncusser*, by Eleanor M. Jewett; the picture on the front of a spooky-looking figure in fishermen's rain gear on the deck of a shipwreck; or the caption that read, "A ghost they said…but was it?" She'd removed it from the shelf for closer inspection, and what she discovered when she opened the cover touched her profoundly. The book was published in 1949, and there was a handwritten note just below the publisher's information, which read,

To my darling daughter Alice, Merry Christmas—1955.

Love, Dad

It was a gift to Grammy from her father. As Robin leafed through the yellowing pages, it was evident this mystery novel had been read numerous times over. The young girl thought of her grandmother, who would have been ten years old at the time of the Christmas gift, and felt as though she was trespassing on a cherished memory. She considered asking her grandmother about it, but quickly decided to try reading the story first. If Grammy had read this book many times, she might gain some insight into her beloved relative as a young girl many decades ago.

At noon, Cresselley grew restless and her stomach was grumbling. She put down "I Am Malala," performed a yoga pose, and cleared her throat. To her astonishment, Robin didn't budge, so she quietly mounted the porch stairs and headed to the kitchen to make a salad.

"What's gotten into your sister?" Carol asked bewildered.

"I have no idea. But it is an enjoyable development, though likely short-term."

"What is she reading that's got her shockingly scholastic out of the blue?"

"You know," Cresselley confessed, "I'm afraid to ask, it might break whatever spell she's under. I think it's an old novel from the living room bookcase. I got a glimpse of the cover and think I recognize it, though I've never actually looked inside. 'Mystery of…'something, I think."

"Aha!" Carol declared, "now it makes sense. That girl has the most energetic imagination I have ever witnessed."

Cresselley thought to herself, *Just wait until midnight*, but said nothing more and left the room.

Out on lawn, tucked in her hammock, Robin was in another world entirely. The main character in her reading was an independent, young girl about her own age named Marty Atwater. She lived in a small fishing village somewhere on the coast of New England with Skipper, her permanently limping little dog and constant companion, as well as her father, the town's sole doctor and on-the-spot veterinarian in a pinch. Her mother had died when Marty was young so her aging, unwed aunt moved in to take on domestic duties. Sadly,

Aunt Eliza was anything but nurturing, and she most definitely did not approve of dogs sharing living spaces with family members.

As Robin read on, she identified more and more intensely with Marty. She was adventurous, inquisitive, and though an only child, she had many friends in the village. Her closest friend, Michael, came from a large family with a long seafaring history. His father had been lost in a storm off the banks while fishing for cod. His grandfather had drifted away from his schooner in a dory in heavy fog, never to be seen again. And his great-grandfather, captain of a schooner heavily loaded with gold from California, lost his life and ship, lured onto the reef by the mooncusser himself (p. 30). Together, they befriended a young blind girl whose much older artist brother and widowed mother had recently bought a small, neglected cottage on the shore. The locals lovingly referred to the bungalow as the Barnacle, acknowledging the little structure's uncanny ability to weather pounding coastal storms.

Robin had never read anything so absorbing. She felt such kinship with the three children whom all, like herself and Elly, had lost a parent at a tender young age. How she longed to reestablish a close relationship with her father like Marty in the book had. And though the village in the book was mostly populated by Portuguese fishing families, the seaside setting had an eerie resemblance to the story of the Allen's, their Grandmother had told them the previous evening.

Robin glanced over at her sister's hammock only to discover it was unoccupied. The sun playing on the water suggested that it was no longer morning. A quick peek at her Fitbit confirmed what Robin suspected, it was afternoon. To be exact, it was 2:00 p.m. and the lunch train had long since left the station. Feeling disorientated in more ways than one, Robin set out to locate her twin. Carol was busy in her room, ironing her freshly washed blouses.

"Do you know where Elly went?"

Carol was startled by Robin's sudden appearance at her door. "Well, look who rejoined reality! I think she's upstairs. We left you the rest of the tuna salad if you're hungry."

"Thanks, Carol, sorry I startled you," the twin added as she bounded up the stairs, two at a time.

Cresselley couldn't fail to notice her sister's approach, so she was surprised when Robin politely announced, "Knock, Knock," before making an entrance.

"Hey, sis, can we talk?" Another out-of-character moment.

"Sure," Cresselley wanted to add "bookworm" to her invitation but refrained.

"About tonight…" Robin hesitated, "you know you're my best friend, and I wouldn't dream of putting you in a dangerous position."

"Oh no, you're not backing out, not after you convinced me you might be right about tonight's opportunity," Cresselley said in a low tone, just in case Carol was in earshot. "What's gotten into you anyway? You're acting weird, like all depsychoed."

"Hey, even I can have a sensitive side. But wait a second, you mean, you *want* to go on the spying mission? I thought you were dead set against it."

"I thought a lot about it after the lunch you missed, and I do think you might be on to something, but there are conditions to my involvement."

"Okay, that's reasonable, go."

"First, I have serious doubts we'll witness any activity around the lake after midnight, unless we stay long enough to catch the pre-dawn 'happy' fishermen. Second, if we don't, it ends there, at least until Jesse gets back or that FBI agent contacts us."

"Fair enough, and if we do spy something suspicious like Britain and Rachael did?"

"Then we'll cautiously see where it leads us."

"You're sure?" Robin felt guilty. Marty would never have pressured her best friend Michael to do something he was apprehensive about.

"You want proof I'm serious? How about this?" Cresselley reached around the side of the bed and held up a pair of dusty binoculars.

"You found some," Robin was flabbergasted.

"They were right where you thought they might be. We should make dinner early, so we can get in a nap before it's time to head up the hill."

"I don't know how I'm going to sleep thinking about all of this and I'll be blasted if I can get that book out of my head, I'm almost finished. And, Elly, I promise to be more considerate of your hesitations in the future. I know I'm impulsive and you are the rational one. It's a balance I need to appreciate."

"I know," Cresselley acknowledged tenderly, "I do too, sis."

Up the Fire Tower

Carol did not join the girls for dinner and though she was bewildered by their early turn in, the whole day had showcased surprising behaviors from both girls. She passed it off as a symptom of the overall impending "teenage affliction." The girls tried their best, but sleep was elusive to both. Robin kept checking her Fitbit, and Cresselley was keenly aware of the ticking, battery-operated clock on the wall two feet from the foot of her bed. The twins remained fully clothed to simplify a hasty, quiet exit. When 11:30 finally rolled around, the girls rendezvoused silently at the top of the stairs. They had agreed in advance that Cresselley would go first and if Carol noticed her, she would say she was on her way to the bathroom and that she had fallen asleep in her clothes, a totally convincing justification for the amenable twin. Cresselley hugged the wall on the way down the stairs, tiptoed by Carol's room, through the inner door, passed the bathroom on the right, the water-skis, kneeboards, and hanging life jackets on the left, and out the screen door into the warm summer night air. She did a pretty good whip-poor-will imitation, so that was the all-clear signal she sent Robin.

Her twin expedited the same course and within a few moments, the girls were side by side in the driveway. They didn't speak until they left the property and headed up the long hill to the fire tower. They kept their flashlights on sparingly to avoid detection, but no cars passed by and the road was void of houses long beyond their destination point. At the top of the hill, they turned right onto the little path that led to the lookout tower, gazing up at the looming structure in the muted moonlight as they approached.

"How old were we when Dad first took us to the top?" Robin asked of her sister's memory.

"Six, maybe… Remember Mom standing at the bottom, watching us climb as though she intended to catch us if we fell?"

"Oh yeah, that's right. I can hear her calling up to Dad the higher we went, 'Robert, this is not a good idea. You bring my girls back down to me this instant.' I recall her saying that about a lot of Dad's activities with us." Robin chuckled. "I wonder what she would say about our own little self-conceived venture in the middle of the night."

"I think she'd have some grim comment about Dad's choice of an adult companion."

Robin suggested ascending first and her sister made no objection. "Wait until I'm on the first landing before you start up," she instructed. "That way if I slip, I won't take you out like a bowling pin."

"Don't say things like that, my nerves are a little brittle at this hour."

"Well, hopefully these nine flights of stairs aren't in that condition. Feels solid, and there's plenty of evidence other trespassers have been here recently. I don't remember this amount of graffiti and beer cans last summer," Robin observed as she rounded the platform and started up the second flight.

They took their time in the dark. It was a sobering experience as they proceeded higher and higher while the abyss below became deeper and blacker. The trees fell away beneath and the bright stars seemed larger with each mounting step.

On the fourth landing, still a level behind her sister, Cresselley did something she had promised herself she would not, under any circumstances, do. She looked down. The twin was well aware of what lay adjacent to the tower, they both were. The girls had explored it many times with their parents, their grandmother, even by themselves. In the bright light of day, it was innocuous and historic, but in the dark shadows, the standing stones appeared sinister and intimidating. It was the Stewart family graveyard.

Robin clearly heard her sister gasp and called down to her in a stern but reassuring voice, "Elly, look up at me. Those people haven't budged in centuries, now climb, one step after the other. We're almost halfway to the top and these rungs are perfectly sound. I'll wait here for you and we can finish the last flights together." In the darkness, Robin couldn't detect her sister's nod, but it was present.

Cresselley began to move again and shortly joined her sister on the fifth landing.

"Sorry, sis, I don't know what possessed me. Snap, wrong word, I don't know what compelled me."

"It's okay, El, I was tempted too… You all right now?"

"Yeah, I'm good. Let's just get there, I want to sit down."

Robin reached the top just ahead of her sister. The trapdoor to the observation cubicle swung wide open, the lock long ago dismantled by some unruly adventure seekers soon after the tower had been decommissioned by the forest service. As her sister came up behind her, Robin reached up and pulled down the short collapsible ladder that enabled access to the observation area, with the final steps. Once in, she extended her hand to give her twin support. The girls sat side by side in the ten-by-ten-foot space feeling accomplished.

"My legs are stinging," Cresselley confessed, "you're a lot more athletic than I am. Yoga possess aren't exactly the equivalent of stair master reps."

Robin chuckled, admiring her sister's candor.

The girls glanced around the interior. It was relatively unchanged since last summer. Most of the removable items had been carried off or tossed over the rail by "meddling kids" decades ago, but some of the equipment used by Mrs. Rathman and the other women who had manned it survived, bolted securely to the structure. The swivel observation chair still worked and though the lens was smashed, the mounted telescope remained—an eerie memento from the original function of the massive, metal tower. In its heyday, there were area maps on the ceiling, a two-way radio, and a little gas stove so Mrs. Rathman and the other women who worked there could make coffee or heat up lunch. The great windows on all sides had little vent systems to let in fresh air, but it wasn't heated, so it stood unmanned in the low fire risk months of winter.

Robert had gone to school with two of the Rathman boys and had been invited to visit the station with them in the ninth grade. That encounter enabled him to give the girls on their first excursion all the way up an accurate description of the operational interior, the equipment, and the importance of the tower before all the modern techniques for fire vigilance went into effect. The state was determined to have it removed and there were rumors in town of an actual buyer who would dismantle it as part of the bargain. The girls were grateful that transaction had not yet occurred and not solely because of the value it had tonight for them, but the family traditions and the history surrounding it.

Robin got up from the bench and sat on the swivel observation chair, gazing out over the vast landscape. Tranquil in its valley, the beloved lake stood out as texture less against the irregular outline of the diverse, tree-lined hills. It was heartening to see from this vantage point the expansiveness of the preserved state forest and all of those beautiful trees so essential to the survival of the planet. Their mother's environmental activism was keenly apparent in her daughters. Without an egotistical, consuming moon, the night sky dazzled imaginative onlookers with a litany of spectacular, "connect the dots" images.

"Elly," Robin whispered, "you awake?"

"I am now," the sister who was groggy responded lightly.

"Do you remember much from those chapters on astronomy other than the North Star and the Big Dipper?"

"I think the constellation 'Scorpion' is visible to us in the summer, but don't ask me to locate it. If you want my opinion, those ancients and mariners had way too much time on their hands at night. I can't pick out any of those archers and bears they saw."

"It must have been like a drive-in theater to them," Robin commented. "You know what would be sweet?"

"Should I be afraid to ask?" Cresselley was fittingly suspicious concerning the practicality of her sister's 'bright ideas,' especially at this hour.

"No, I think you'll actually like this one. Carol wants us to come up with ideas for outings, let's ask her to drop us off at the Mystic Seaport Museum one afternoon. We can go to their planetarium show about the seasonal night sky. I'm pretty sure it runs daily all summer."

"I am astonished," Cresselley admitted, "that's an awesome idea. Have you seen any activity out there yet other than a star show? I can take over the watch. What time is it anyway?"

Robin glanced at her wrist. "1:15," she reported. "You're probably right about this excursion being ludicrous."

"Hey, we're here, I'll start paying attention."

"Take the chair, Elly, I need to stretch." Robin stood up and raised her hands over her head, bending left then right at the waist.

"So which direction do you think the bear cave is in?"

"Remember when we took compass readings off Dad's map?"

Cresselley nodded to her sister.

"Well, if those were correct, the bear cave should be right over there, halfway up that hill you can just see outlined by the dark sky," Robin pointed. "And that seems reasonable to me, the north shore of the lake where the dirt of Murray Road ends and the 'no trespassing' signs are is approximately the same heading."

"I see it now," Cresselley's excitement mounted, "and that would be the boat launch way over to the left."

"Exactly, and the old logging road we took from the Chapman cemetery is in the opposite direction, off to the right. Any movement of lights in those areas we can easily spot. The only other real trail on that side of the lake heads off to the north, out of our direct line of sight."

"It makes so much more sense when you look at the geography from this height," Cresselley again admired her sister's sense of direction and positioning. "I can see how you think these locations could be connected."

The girls kept their lookout for another half an hour, when Cresselley got her sister's attention. "Robbie," she whispered, "look over at the north end, there's moving lights."

Robin turned her concentration to where her sister had indicated. "You're right. Those are car headlights coming up the dead-end dirt road. Remember what Grammy said about Mrs. Hui, the lady who lives in the brown house near the end, right across from where the birthday party was?"

"I think she said she is an operating room nurse at the hospital."

"That's it, and she told us that Mrs. Hui sometimes works odd hours to set up for the 6:00 a.m. surgeries. I bet that's her leaving for work. If I'm right, that car should pass by on the road below us in about four minutes," Robin estimated.

Sure enough, the headlights disappeared momentarily as the car climbed the hill along the same route the girls had taken just a few hours ago and minutes later with its sole occupant, passed below the tower where the girls were engaged in surveillance.

"Have a nice shift, Mrs. Hui. And thank you for your service," Robin whispered.

"You silly." Cresselley nudged her sister affectionately.

Another half an hour passed, and Robin's breathing suggested she was dozing in an upright position.

Cresselley did not wake her. She thought silently, *Let her rest for now, this is an opportunity to prove that I'm one hundred percent with her in this covert escapade.*

The consideration had barely left the young girl's mind when a faint light appeared at the estimated cave location. Cresselley held her breath, waiting for confirmation. Sure enough, a minute later, two more lights became visible, followed closely by a fourth. The exact number of sleeping bags they had discovered. As they began to move, she gently shook her sister.

"I'm awake. I'm awake. Something happening?"

"Look," her twin directed, "moving lights, four of them."

Robin sat up straight and took the binoculars Cresselley handed her. "They're right where we thought. It looks as though they're headed toward the shoreline."

"Well, good luck to them if they think they can get through on that side. Remember when we tried to get to the boat launch from the end of the dirt road?"

"Boy, do I," Robin agreed, "it was brutal in daylight. Imagine what it's like with a flashlight."

"We got so scratched up plowing through the briars and bittersweet."

It wasn't a pleasant memory for either of the twins and one ramble they never attempted again. It was an undeveloped area of the lake where the state forest bordered the land trust and where this flashlight troop seemed to be headed, rough terrain.

"Let's see what they do. They might turn back. Doesn't it seem odd how one of them is out in front, there are two clustered in the middle, and the fourth sort of bringing up the rear?" Robin questioned.

"They look like rustlers, moving stolen horses." Cresselley's analogy made Robin giggle, but it was the precise concept she was having trouble articulating.

The pace of "the suspects" surprised the girls. They were quickly closing in on the eastern end of the darkened boat launch.

"Maybe they did some clearing in anticipation of tonight's outing," Cresselley speculated.

"Or they've made this 'run' on other occasions," Robin added. She had scarcely finished her sentence when headlights appeared on the hill above the launch and marked a vehicle's final decent to the parking lot where the road ended abruptly. It turned in and dowsed all lights. "This cannot be a coincidence," Robin declared with unflinching certainty. "And that's no fisherman. We would have spotted boat trailer running lights."

"And the plot thickens," Cresselley sounded like she was being sarcastic, when in fact, she was serious.

The four flashlights drew up to the last known location of the car and two of them were extinguished. A fresh light ignited in what appeared through the binoculars to be the back of the car.

"What on earth is this latest development?" Cresselley was mystified.

"I think someone opened the trunk."

The girl's eyes met uneasily.

Before Robin could speculate further, the light went out and the car sped away, its red taillights vanishing into the dark as it rounded the corner at the crest of the hill. The girls sat speechless until it became evident two of the flashlight bearers had remained behind.

"Let me have a go at the binoculars," Cresselley enticed.

"Sure, sorry I've been hogging them."

As Cresselley put the glasses to her face, the handheld lights were on the move yet again.

"They're not headed back," she informed her sister.

"I can tell that much, but what could possibly be of interest in the woods to the west of the boat ramp? Can you see what they're up to?"

"Well, they went a short distance into the trees and stopped. I might be interpreting their behavior wrong, but I'd say they're looking for something. Here, you look." Cresselley handed the binoculars back to her twin.

Robin took a long, silent gaze into the lens.

"Don't keep me in suspense, any theories?"

Robin sat back down on the swivel chair and contemplated before answering. Cresselley recognized the look on her sister's face and waited patiently. Pressuring wouldn't speed up the process.

In due course, Robin leaned forward and addressed her companion, "Do you remember that Boy Scout dude in science class last spring?"

"You mean Ian Brown with the 'dreamy' eyes?"

"Elly, focus"—Robin rolled her eyes—"He talked about this online thing where you got compass headings and miscellaneous other directions then you went to find a specific spot?"

"Oh yeah," Cresselley did remember. "Didn't he explain that you found a buried box or something that had registration papers you could write on to prove you'd been successful?"

"That's how I understood it too. If I remember correctly, he told the class there were seven of those destinations right here in town. Maybe one of them is by the boat launch where that duo is up to something, they want no one else to see."

What Robin was suggesting made good sense to Cresselley. "If we go to the library tomorrow, oh wait, it is tomorrow, later today then, we can go online and look for the information about that competition. If the boy scouts can figure it out, we sure can."

The girls looked up to see if there was a retreat going on by the shoreline. The flashlight dyad was moving fast. They had almost made it to the turnoff leading back to the cave. The girls watched silently, waiting to see if they would make the turn, they didn't.

"Okay, they only really have two choices, dirt Murray Road, where they'd have to pass by several occupied cottages, or head out the old logging trail we took to the cave that first day we met Jesse."

Cresselley listened attentively to her sister's deductions and added insightfully, "We accessed that trail by way of the Chapman Cemetery. Jesse said that's where he saw the parked car late one night. Maybe they have a ride waiting for them."

"I agree completely," Robin's approval was a noteworthy complement to her sister.

"There are just a few things I'm curious about, Detective."

"Yes, Agent," Robin played along.

"About the box, if that's some sort of contact thing, why not just use cell phones?"

"That's easy," Robin replied, "we know how lousy service is here, but also, if the authorities get onto them, they can be traced through GPS or cell phone towers. In addition, the content of those calls or texts can be accessed."

"You really have watched massive amounts of CSI whatever."

"It's paying off, was there something else?"

"I'm still not clear on exactly how the box might fit in?"

"What if they leave coded messages and that's how they arranged the rendezvous with the car that showed up tonight."

"Seems like a lot of trouble to go to."

"Not if the payoff is big enough. Whatever they're up to, they sure don't want to get caught," Robin observed. Looking for the letterbox would be a legitimate explanation for them if they were noticed in the woods at night. "And that was definitely a transfer of some kind tonight."

The sky was beginning to brighten in the pre-dawn hour. Suddenly, the moving lights disappeared.

"Where could they have gone?" Cresselley was perplexed. "I haven't taken my eyes off them since they bypassed the trail to the cave."

"They're still out there making their way up the hill," her sister assured her. "They turned their flashlights off, it's light enough to travel without them now and it's also light enough for us to head home to the cottage. We won't see any more activity tonight."

"I'm definitely good with that."

The scale down the tower, though not effortless, was much quicker. It didn't take long for the girls to get to the last landing. Cresselley looked down over the railing before descending the final flight.

"I like all of you much better in the daylight," she whispered down. "Rest in peace, you Stewarts. We'll be seeing you!"

"You're a nut," her sister commented lightly.

It was just about 5:00 a.m. when the girls turned into the driveway.

"Let's go through the screen door on the lakeside porch," Robin proposed. "That way, we can get upstairs without passing Carol's room."

"Good idea, sis. Wonder why we didn't think of that last night."

Though their minds were still racing, the girls were physically exhausted. Robin kicked off her shoes, tossed her socks at the laundry basket, missed but fell into bed and pulled the covers over her head despite the miscalculation. She'd clean the room and change her clothes later in the day. Cresselley really wanted a shower, but she disrobed, pulled a clean nightshirt over her head, and collapsed into bed.

The Library

Neither twin stirred until ten o'clock. It was a beautiful day.

"I'm famished," Robin growled as the girls entered the kitchen. "I don't have time for any fancy prep work this morning. Did Grammy give us any of those little mouse-portion-size, single-serving, cold cereal boxes? Do you know, Elly?"

"You're such a bear when you're hungry. Look in the storage bin under the chopping block."

Cresselley hoped their grandmother had not assumed they were too old for the tiny cereal boxes; even though Robin was right, they were no bigger than sample size.

"Oh, thank you, Gram. It's going to take about three of these little babies, so which ones might mix well?" Robin had opened the top and was staring into the bin. "Let's see here, we can put together apple jacks, frosted flakes, and cocoa puffs, perfect! Now, just a monster bowl, a little cow juice, and voila, breakfast!" Robin blew past her sister, stopping for a brief second on her way to the porch at the hutch in the dining area for a large serving spoon. "Su-ga, su-ga," she chanted gutturally all the way to the table.

Little did she know, her food critic twin was in front of the refrigerator doubled over laugh-crying at her sister's antics. When she finally stood up straight again, she put two slices of wheat bread in the toaster and pushed the "down" lever. Then she picked up the fruit bowl, poured a glass of orange juice, and followed her sister to the porch.

"Would you like a glass of OJ?" she asked Robin, who had almost finished the giant bowl of cereal.

She had the basin in her hands, tipping it back to her mouth, slurping the remaining flavorful milk. "No, I'm good," she responded as the liquid dripped down her shirt. "Hey, you all right?" her sister looked as though she had been crying, but the grin on her face was broad.

"I'm fine, how about a banana to go with that sludge?" Cresselley couldn't contain herself any longer. She burst out laughing, spraying her dumbfounded twin with orange juice mist.

It was too much for either of them, they simultaneously doubled over the table in unmanageable hysterics.

Out on the dock, Carol heard the rumpus and came through the screen door.

"What on earth are you girls…what's that smell?"

The girls looked up to see black smoke spilling into the dining area. The sight of what was coming out of the kitchen just set the girls deeper into fits of hilarity.

"Hey, El, think your toast is done?" Robin could barely catch her breath, but she managed to get the words out. "Bet you forgot Gram's toaster hasn't popped up automatically in two years."

Now Carol was laughing deafeningly right along with her charges and to punctuate the moment, the smoke detector began its cautionary blare. And the final icing on the cake, Mrs. Mote, appeared at the screen door to inquire if everything was all right. She had a land line and could phone the volunteer fire company, the paramedics, or both if necessary. Composing herself, Carol thanked the neighbor and assured her all was as it should be, whatever that was.

"Well, girls, I'm glad to see you're out of whatever put you in such a solemn state for the past few days. Is there anything special you would like to do today?"

"Can you drop us at the library? And when we're finished, we'll walk to the post office, we promised to drop in on Gram."

"Sure, I'll go for groceries while you're busy."

"Are you still taking tomorrow off, Carol?" Cresselley was thinking ahead.

"I was planning on it, Louis wants to take me to see the 'Breakers' mansion in Newport, so I might be really late. Do you think your grandmother will mind staying that long?"

"No," Cresselley was certain, "she won't mind. We'll convince her to just stay overnight with us, so you don't have to worry about the hour."

"That's very sweet of you girls, thank you."

Forty-five minutes later, Carol with the girls in the back seat, pulled up in front of the library. It was one of the oldest municipal buildings in town, originally constructed in 1900 as a private boarding school with dormitories on its grounds, classrooms on the first floor, and a carpentry shop in the basement. The colossal granite building had been absorbed into the town's formal public-school system, constructed on the same acreage in 1950, several years after the departure of the long-standing private facility. Their grandmother recalled weekly "field trips" to the library as a grammar school student. She also remembered fondly the librarian who selected a book to read out loud to the class of budding academics in a circle at her feet every Thursday at 10:00 a.m. and how exhausting the climb up the long staircase to the second floor seemed to a first grader. The girls loved this old, majestic structure now completely devoted to the town's library.

"I'll pick you up at the post office at 1:30, okay?" Carol inquired of the girls as they stepped out of the little Prius.

"That's fine," Robin agreed. "Hey, Carol, when you go to the store, can you pick up a big box of Frosted Mini-Wheat's?"

Carol and Cresselley exchanged perceptive glances prior to the purchaser agreeing to the request with the hint of a smile.

"Before we go in, how do you want to work this?" Robin asked her fellow detective.

"Since you know more about the geography and map coordinates, why don't you look at the website for possible matches to the lake area, I'll check on the school's website for a suggested summer reading list and pick something out. That way, we're able to legitimize the visit if anyone asks."

"Good strategy, Agent," Robin praised.

It didn't take long for her to locate the website for the activity their classmate had made them aware of, and the boy scout was correct, there were seven specific destinations here in town. It was called

"Letterbox" and there were directions for finding each of the sites. Now she just needed to locate coordinates that might indicate an area near the boat launch, there were two. She could make copies of the information for ten cents a page and given the absence of Wi-Fi at the lake, she was grateful to take that option.

Meanwhile, Cresselley had pulled up the school webpage and made a copy of book titles for eighth grade summer reading: "Fahrenheit 451," "The Outsiders," "The Yearling," the Harry Potter series, "Short Stories of Edgar Allen Poe," "Summer of Monkeys." There was also a section entitled, "For advanced readers who like a challenge," and one of the selections listed there caught her attention. It was a recent paperback she had overheard her father discussing, "Promise Me, Dad," by Joseph Biden. She decided to see if the library possessed a copy and if so, was it in. In addition, she tracked down a copy of "Fahrenheit 451" for backup. Cresselley was an avid reader all year long and without formal coursework, she could easily devour three or four books a week during summer vacation. This season, however, was shaping up to be an exception. If they didn't solve or settle this mystery business soon, she'd be lucky to have any of the reading list completed before school resumed.

She went to the desk to check out. Amy, the head librarian, was impressed that a middle school reader was interested in Biden's book, but the library's copy was out. She offered to check interlibrary loan for Cresselley then added, "I saw it for sale in Drew's front window the other day, maybe you would like to own it."

"Thanks, Amy"—the twin smiled—"that's actually a wonderful suggestion." She checked out the other book and considered asking her father if he had an opinion about her reading the Biden title.

Cresselley glanced over to the computer corner, but her sister was no longer there. Assuming Robin had finished her research, she exited through the heavy doors and into the sunny afternoon.

"Hey Robbie, did you find what you were looking for?"

"I did, and this shouldn't be too complicated. We think we know where the approximate location is, so we can skip over all the clues that guide sleuths to the lake. All we need to do is solve the last piece of the scavenger hunt, and I bet we can accomplish that this afternoon. The directions say to bring your own inkpad and personal stamp to mark your triumph, but we don't need all that. We just want a look at what might be inside the box. What book did you pick out?"

Cresselley held the text up so that her sister could read the title.

"'Fahrenheit 451,'" Robin looked puzzled. "What is that?"

"It's the temperature that books burn at," her twin explained. "Why don't you read it when I'm finished," Cresselley taunted.

"Maybe I will, Miss Smarty. It's ten after one, we need to get to the post office if we're going to have time to speak to Gram."

The girls departed the formidable library steps and headed out on the short walk to where their grandmother worked. She observed their approach and met them at the counter.

"There are my lovely granddaughters. How was the library and Amy?"

"Great, Gram," Robin spoke first.

"Carol won't be back tomorrow night until pretty late, Grammy," Cresselley was fulfilling her promise. "I can sleep in my old single bed in Robin's room and you could have your old big bedroom back. Then you could stay overnight and not be tired for work the following morning."

"That's very thoughtful of you, dear. I'll put together an overnight bag, so I can dress for work at the cottage. You can relay this to Carol?"

"Oh, yes."

"And guess who just pulled up out front," Robin observed. "Bye, Gram, see you tomorrow."

"Hey, my lovelies, before you run off, how about I bring a pizza for dinner? If you feel like cooking, you can always prepare dessert."

"Thanks, Gram, great idea," Robin agreed.

Pizza sounded like a sinful respite from the healthy food menu Cresselley had regimented for the girls.

"Gram's on board for tomorrow's slumber party," Cresselley reported to Carol as she slid onto the back seat of the little hybrid.

Letterbox

It was marginally too late for the twins to kayak to the boat launch, scout for the letterbox, and paddle back to the cottage without drawing suspicion from Carol, so the girls decided to postpone their latest plans until the next day. It was just as well. As eager as Robin was to solve this next piece of the mysterious puzzle, the delay afforded her extra time to decipher the exact location of the letterbox and accelerate their search for the spot the next day.

Eager to continue their quest, the girls were in their kayaks headed toward the boat launch soon after sunrise. The parking lot was empty as they beached their crafts and marched into the woods to the left of the pavement. Robin had studied the online instructions in great depth and led the way counting their steps out loud. Minutes later, she paused.

"We should be about on top of the letterbox," she informed Cresselley. "Look for a spot that might have been disturbed recently."

"Here, Robbie. These leaves look deliberately arranged." Cresselley knelt down and began pushing aside the pile of decay, her sister joined her.

"Nice work, Agent," Robin complimented. She tapped on what sounded like metal just below the surface.

Together, the girls pulled a square box from its shallow grave. With keen expectation, they opened the lid and peered inside. There were a variety of ink stamps and short messages in a notebook, but nothing that appeared out of the ordinary or suspicious.

"That's disappointing." Cresselley sighed.

But Robin wasn't ready to give up, sure her theory about coded messages had merit. Turning the box over, she tapped on the bottom with her index finger.

"I think there is a false bottom if I can just figure out how to access it."

"Let me try," Cresselley suggested. "My nails are longer."

To Robin's delight, the bottom slid open under Cresselley's command. Together, the girls looked inside the narrow square and pulled out a folded sheet of paper.

"You look," Cresselley proposed, "you're the one who figured this out."

Just as Robin did so, the sound of a truck backing into the boat launch broke the early morning quiet.

"Whoever it is will see the kayaks and wonder where the paddlers are," Cresselley said nervously.

"I brought my cell," Robin admitted. "I'll take some pictures and put the whole thing back. You can stroll out and make a presence. I'm in the latrine."

Cresselley nodded in approval and left Robin with the letterbox.

"Good morning, Officer Mendez," Cresselley greeted. "Getting in some fishing?"

"Hello there, young lady, where is your partner in crime this early hour?" the smiling officer questioned.

"She'll be along in a minute. Going solo this time?"

"Well, apparently once a daughter turns thirteen, it is no longer cool to go fishing with your dad. I'm going to back up the truck and get the boat in the water. Can you let me know when it floats, Cresselley? It would be a big help!"

"Sure, I'd be glad to."

Officer Mendez climbed up into the cab of his red, four-wheel-drive truck and slowly backed the boat trailer down the ramp. When the little craft began to float, Cresselley shouted to him. He got out, went knee deep in the water, and pushed the boat off its trailer.

"I'll hold the bowline while you park the truck," Cresselley offered, just as Robin appeared from the trees.

"There you are, Robin. I've never known the two of you to be more than a few feet from each other. Your sister has kindly been assisting me with a launch."

"It's a fine morning to catch a trout," Robin offered awkwardly. She knew she should leave it at that, but the temptation was stronger than her judgment. "The Chapman girls told us they reported activity at the end of Murray road and up by the bear cave," she boldly added.

"They did," Officer Mendez reported. "I checked out the tire tracks that afternoon and last night, I paid a surprise visit to the cave."

"Did you find anything?" Robin pursued.

"Not even a bear." Officer Mendez chuckled. "But I still want you girls to stay clear of the woods. Your dad is concerned about your little excursions."

"Just water sports," Cresselley said politely. "Can we push you off? I'm sure you're eager to get out there."

Officer Mendez smiled. "Trying to get rid of me? That's okay, girls. Have a great day and give my regards to your father." With that, he started the little motor and waved goodbye.

"Can't believe he didn't see anything in or on the way to the cave," Robin sounded suspicious.

"Maybe they moved to another location," Cresselley offered. "Things must be heating up for them or they never would have sent us the note in the restaurant."

"I bet they're still in the area though, otherwise Officer Mendez wouldn't have warned us about trail hikes. I wonder if he knows anything about the state forest between here and Cassidy Hill."

"I thought of that too," Robin admitted. "But asking would have raised his suspicions without giving us any info."

"So the bird in the hand. What did the paper in the box say?" Cresselley continued.

"It looks like code all right," Robin confirmed. "I got a good picture of it. Let's go back to the cottage and see how good we are at decrypting."

On the dock, pouring over the image on Robin's cellphone with so much interest, the twins failed to notice Carol's approach.

"What are you two studying with such intensity?" she whispered, startling the girls.

"It's a kind of puzzle we got off the internet at the library," Robin offered a selective explanation.

"I'm good at puzzles, let me see."

Reluctantly, Robin handed Carol her cell.

"Numbers, okay. Looks like a date, 0701, and maybe a time."

"That's what we thought too," Cresselley ventured. "But what's the 'z'?"

"So 1700z," Carol read. "That's Zulu time."

"Translation please," Robin implored.

"It's Greenwich, England, time. Remember when I dated that pilot for a few months? He taught me. It's what pilots reference. So seventeen hundred hours would be seven p.m. in Greenwich, and since we are on daylight savings time, that would be two in the afternoon here."

"Awesome, Carol, who knew," Robin commented unsarcastically.

"You're on your own with the last of it though. I have no idea what XRD could possibly be."

"No worries, you've been a great help," Cresselley complimented.

"Well, if you girls win anything from the decoding, I want a third!" Their companion laughed as she retreated to the cottage.

"You got it!"

At the sound of the screen door, Robin looked over at her sister. "Are you thinking what I am, XRD?"

"Crossroads," Cresselley barely whispered.

"How many times have we heard that place mentioned this summer? It has to be involved in some way."

"We need to find someone who'll tell us about it," Cresselley admitted. "I doubt we'll get anything out of Gram, after the way she acted when we asked the other night."

"We can't question Dad either, he'll get all suspicious, especially since now we know he did call Officer Mendez."

"I wonder if Jesse's Dad knows."

"Even if he does, it'll be too late by the time they get back. July first is the day after tomorrow."

"The FBI agent couldn't find any written historical piece about it."

"We'll think of something, my brain is tired," Robin admitted.

"That's a first. Let's flush our heads reading in our hammocks like we did before the fire tower excursion."

A Precious Gift

The girls got up to greet Louis when he picked up Carol midafternoon, complimenting him on the restaurant. Their grandmother arrived at six o'clock, pizza in hand as promised.

"I have a surprise gift for you girls after dinner," she hinted.

"Tell us, Gram, we're terrible at waiting," the twins implored.

"Very well, I don't want you choking on green papers. I know you girls have seen the photos from your parents' wedding, but they declined my offer for a professional video."

"Grammy, you didn't!"

"I most certainly did! It was filmed on what was then the newest equipment, of course, terribly outdated now that anyone can film with their phone. The technical problem is you can't play it without the camera and all of the hookups for the TV."

The girls looked disappointed and their grandmother smiled.

"But," she continued, "my young, co-worker, Amira, told me about a new business in the borough's old Velvet Mill that can digitize anything and even put it on a DVD." As she finished the last sentence, their grandmother reached in her shoulder bag and pulled out a flat, black case. "I thought you girls should have it."

Cresselley looked close to tears.

"Now that's what I don't want," their grandmother confessed. "If watching this will make you sad…"

"Gram, I'm blurry-eyed happy," the young girl insisted. "Can we put it in the player?"

Robin had already side-stepped permission. The screen on the old TV came to life and the title read, "Margaret and Robert, June

21, 1998." The clip went directly to the Justice of the Peace officiated ceremony on their grandmother's lawn with a large, white tent in the background.

"Look at Mom," Robin whispered, "so young, beautiful, happy, and alive." She almost regretted voicing her last observation, but everyone agreed.

Following the short ceremony, the receiving line came into view.

"Isn't that Mom's college roommate?" Cresselley questioned.

"Isn't she lovely," Grandmother noted.

Suddenly, Robin sat up staring with deep concentration at the screen.

"Gram, do you know who that guy is?" Indicating a figure shaking their father's hand. "The one with the lion's head tattoo on his inner arm?"

"I believe he's one of the Lewis boys. I'm not sure which one, there were four."

"That's a pretty distinctive tat."

"Many of your father's friends had them."

"What was up with that?" Robin wasn't letting it go until she had a full explanation.

"It was rather foolish in my opinion," Grandmother scolded. "It was a tradition with the soccer team players. I don't know how it got started, but when the town hired a new coach, he put a stop to it."

"But Dad was on the soccer team, and he doesn't have one," Cresselley observed.

"He wanted one. Fortunately, I talked him out of it."

"How did you do that, Gram? We've never changed his mind on anything."

"First of all, he was a minor, of course, so were the rest of his teammates. More importantly for my objection, your father wanted to be a lawyer since he read 'Gideon's Trumpet' in the seventh grade. I pointed out to him that he'd only have a few years on the soccer team and it wouldn't look very professional in his chosen career."

"So how many players do you think got them, Gram?" Robin followed up.

"It went on for about a four-year period, I'd guess maybe nine or so. The team never had more than sixteen members in any given year and many of the parents refused to give permission for it."

"Interesting," Robin was secretly exalted but dropped the subject. "Hey, isn't that Charlie Smyth dancing with Mom?"

"By golly, it is," Grandmother confirmed. "Do you girls remember visiting him with your parents in his home by the boat launch? You should drop in on him this summer. He's the unofficial town historian and does he love to tell stories."

"That's a great idea, Gram," Cresselley said. "We'll go tomorrow."

The last scene on the DVD was their smiling parents waving goodbye to their guests from a red convertible.

The room was quiet for several minutes in reflective thought. It was Grandmother who broke the silence.

She began in a soft voice, "You girls have no idea how proud I am of how well you have handled the loss of your precious mother." She paused briefly then added, "Particularly considering the circumstances."

The twins stood and embraced their loving grandmother.

"She was doing something she was passionate about," Cresselley whispered.

"Good night, my darlings."

The twins heard the bedroom door close and sat for a moment. It was Robin, this time, who broke the quiet and deliberately changed the tone.

"This makes so much sense," Robin interpreted the content of the video. "Of course, there had to be a local involved. How else would the offenders know about the bear cave, the cemetery, even the Barkers being out of town? It doesn't tell us who exactly, but this sure narrows it down. Maybe if we look again at Dad's yearbook and check out the soccer team, we might narrow down the dude from the restaurant. They can't all be tall with brown hair."

Cresselley nodded and stood. "Here we thought we'd never get anything from Gram about the Crossroads, and she handed us the perfect source. We should go to bed too, Robbie. Gram won't sleep until she hears us come up."

Charlie's History Lesson

Their Grandmother had already turned in when the girls got to the top of the stairs. They continued to whisper, sitting on Cresselley's old single bed, away from the thin wall.

"Let's go see Charlie first thing in the morning. Do you think he joins the men's coffee club at Drew's?" Robin wondered.

"I wouldn't be surprised." Cresselley stifled a chuckle. "He meets the age and residency requirements."

The sound of a car door and distant voices alerted the girls of Carol's return.

"We better get some sleep too."

"How crazy exciting," Robin gushed. "We probably should wait until ten o'clock tomorrow to give the duffer club time to wrap it up."

"Shouldn't we try to get a hold of Jesse?"

"We'll either have a lot or nothing to tell him, El. He'll be back before we know it."

Their grandmother's bed was made and her car wasn't in the driveway when the girls got up the next morning. To their surprise, however, Carol was reading the morning paper at the dining area table.

"You're up early," Robin commented.

"How was Newport?" Cresselley asked politely.

"Lavish and historic," Carol offered. "Hey, girls, there's a brief article in today's region section about a volunteer day at the horse rescue farm in town, interested?"

"For sure, we joined the volunteer club at school, but they don't have formal activities over vacation," Robin informed.

"Great, Sunday afternoon then."

There was a note from their grandmother on the kitchen counter, "Take some of our jam to Charlie, he's a big fan. Love you!"

At nine thirty, jam in hand, the girls kayaked in the direction of the boat launch once again. Approaching, the twins could see Charlie's car parked in the driveway and as they beached their boats, the man himself waved from his overhead porch.

"My goodness, are my eyes deceiving me or can it be the Spenser twins have come for a visit?" he called down over the railing. "You girls are getting so grown up, I barely recognize you. Come on up and tell me to what I owe this call on such a lovely morning."

The girls bounded up the porch stairs and Charlie's adorable cocker spaniel, Taffy, sprinted down to them, wagging her tail. The view of the lake from the porch was remarkable, with direct sunlight both morning and evening.

"We're so happy we caught you at home," Cresselley said with sincerity as she handed over the jam.

"Sweet, strawberry, let me guess, you and your grandmother picked at Maple Acres a few weeks ago."

"We did." Robin smiled.

"So what can I do for you young ladies this morning? I'm sure there is more than jam behind your attention to an old man."

Without a hint of denial Robin began, "Gram told us you are the unofficial historian of all things North Milltown."

"Well, if living here for seven and a half decades qualifies me, then yes, you could say that."

"We were wondering what you can tell us about 'the Crossroads.'"

"Well, I'll be…," Charlie mused. "I haven't heard mention of that place for a month of Sundays. What on earth has you girls all fired up about it?"

"Dad promised to take us there before the summer is over, so we were curious."

"Well, your dad's generation is undoubtably the last group of teenagers to have any knowledge of it, let alone explore the location."

"We suspect the trail is somewhere across from the boat launch. Gram said she'd be surprised if Dad could even find it again because it's all overgrown."

"That's true," Charlie agreed. "But anyone who knows what to look for could probably manage. I haven't been back there in about five years since my arthritis caught up with me. It's a pretty lengthy hike with all sorts of brambles and bittersweet."

"Tell us about it," the girls begged.

"Are you sure you don't want to wait for your dad? He might prefer to be the historian."

"Pretty please. There isn't any information about it in the library."

"Not surprising, I doubt there are actual records anywhere. There was a great deal of controversy surrounding the compound, particularly during prohibition. Get comfortable, girls, if you really want to hear the whole story. By golly, it could pass as one of Chaucer's tales. Lemonade, iced tea?"

"We're good," Robin was quick to respond as the girls took seats on the long, padded porch swing.

"How about you, Taffy? You good?" Charlie reached down and stroked the cocker spaniel's long, soft ears. He leaned back in his recliner with a wistful look and began. "I'm sure you girls are aware that this whole area of eastern Connecticut and into Rhode Island was at one time dotted with mills, mostly textile, beginning sometime around the civil war. Well, the Crossroads is exactly what it sounds like, the intersection of two important commerce roads, one ran north–south, the other east–west. Of course, this was before there were gas-powered vehicles. It was all horse drawn back then. In the beginning, much of the traffic had to do with commercial trans-actions between the mills. My grandfather, Niles Smyth, was born in 1890 and as young man, he was a part-time courier for the mill in the borough."

"The Velvet Mill," Robin politely interrupted.

"Yes, precisely," Charlie affirmed. "And it's a good example of one structure that survived and was refitted to accommodate small businesses. Many of the brick structures did survive, though the wooden ones either rotted or were targeted by arsons. My grandfather told me many stories about the Crossroads. It had already been in operation for a number of years before he began working full time for a big thread mill up in Staffville."

"So what was it exactly, Charlie, a night club?" Robin couldn't contain herself.

Charlie laughed patiently. "You're pretty close," he encouraged. "It was a stopping-off point for travelers making the long journey between the mills and other miscellaneous guests. By the time my grandfather began stopping on a regular basis, it was a booming, practically self-sustaining oasis. The central focus was a large inn—the top two floors for overnight guests, the first floor for what I imagine would have been referred to at the time as a saloon. There were poker tables, a bar, and sections where they served food from a large kitchen in the back. In support, there was a massive barn where the guests could have their horse teams overnighted or a midday feed and watering. There was also a chicken coop, a pig pen, cows and goats for milk, cheese, and butter production, a large vegetable garden, and quite famously a sizable apple orchard."

"What made the apple orchard famous?" Cresselley was just as captivated as her spellbound twin.

"The owners made apple cider from the drops and seconds, which they stored in large kegs in the inn's dirt basement. In time, the cider turned into alcohol or 'hard cider' which was a favorite with the patrons. Sometime around 1915, a couple from the Netherlands fled the Great War and purchased the compound, officially naming it Dutch Village. When prohibition became the law of the land five years later, they quickly realized there was a great deal of money to be made through the prohibited sale of alcohol. They welcomed bootlegging traffickers and hosted a variety of other questionable activities, a few not appropriate for discussion in present company. Local law enforcement not only looked the other way but were regulars at what had become a popular 'watering hole.' I'm sure the temperance supporters weren't enchanted with the idea, but it was out of sight and the owners were really very lovely people."

"When did it close down?" Wide-eyed Robin inquired.

"There were contributing factors to its demise," Charlie recollected. "The second world war drained this area, as well as the rest of the country of men, the textile industry moved south, and prohibition ended in 1933. History remembers those thirteen plus years as a failed experiment, contributing more to crime than preventing it. The last nail in its coffin, the couple who owned it, abandoned ship and returned to their home country."

"Didn't they sell it?"

"Couldn't, it wasn't worth anything once new paved roads went in bypassing it altogether. I think the taxes were paid up for a few years, but once that ran out, it became the property of the town. Eventually, the first selectman, Alfred Crofts, Sr., ordered no trespassing signs enforced. Once it went into decay, the place became a liability for the taxpayers. They couldn't afford to clear the old road to accommodate the massive equipment needed to demolish the remaining structures, that kind of expenditure would never have been approved in the town's budget."

"Did you ever visit when it was in operation?" Robin asked with some hesitation.

"I am an old man"—Charlie chuckled—"not a fossil. My father did take me as a youngster. It was abandoned by then, but still intact. Very ghostly if I had to describe it."

"What's left now?" The term "ghostly" troubled Cresselley.

"Not much of the inn. The front wall still stands and the framing for the big windows on all three levels. If you look closely, there are a few remaining wooden kegs in the basement, there's nothing left of the flooring above where the serving area was. The last time I hiked in, the little apartment added on at the back of the kitchen appeared as though with a little tidying up, you could move right in."

"Sad," Robin remarked. "What about the outbuildings?"

"The barn remains, I wouldn't put a horse in it. The chicken coop is a pile of debris. You still get a sense of the layout though, despite all the overgrowth. The town was wise to let it fall out of memory, it's a dangerous place to poke around in. Don't you girls make me sorry I told you all of this. If your dad decides to take you, wonderful, but it's no place for adventure seekers."

"Thank you, Charlie, for the history lesson. We're sure Dad would never remember or even know most of it. We just hope he can find it again," Robin hinted.

"Remind him about twenty paces past the boat launch on the opposite side of the road, a large boulder marks the original access trail. Head west until you intercept the old north-south road. It's not a clear route anymore, but parallel stonewalls visibly map it. Just track between them until you reach what's left of the compound. He'll recognize it, girls."

The twins prepared to leave with a pat on Taffy's head.

"Bye, Charlie, we'll come back again for another visit. Next time, we'll bring blueberries, they're just beginning to ripen on the islands."

"Give my best to your grandmother." Charlie waved as the twins launched their kayaks and embarked on the paddle home.

With her imagination in overdrive, Robin soon fell well behind Cresselley. "El, wait up," she shouted.

Her twin turned around, noted the distance between them and rested on her paddle. Robin quickly came alongside and held the boats together.

"I'll go tomorrow," she announced. "You stay at the cottage. That way, if I don't get back by four o'clock, you can alert Officer Mendez."

"Oh right, Carol would never be suspicious. You think I can just hang out and not go stir crazy."

"You can think of something to reassure her. Tell her we had a fight and needed some time out. Finish 'Fahrenheit 451.'"

"Seriously? There is no way I'm missing out. I want to solve this thing as much as you do. Besides, you need someone along to monitor your impulsiveness."

"I won't get close if someone shows up," Robin promised. "I'll stay hidden and use the binoculars."

"We'll stay hidden," Cresselley underscored.

"Okay, I just thought I'd give you a pass."

"You figured you could get all the credit and impress Jesse."

"Dad, maybe." Robin grinned. "All right, you win. We'll head out right after lunch and tie the kayaks to the bushes at the boat launch. That should get us there before the two o'clock rendezvous in the coded message."

Carol had take-out Chinese waiting on the picnic table when the girls returned. "How was your visit with Charlie?" she asked. "He is such a nice man."

"His stories are awesome," Robin acknowledged with enthusiasm. "Shrimp egg rolls, cool! Thanks, Carol! So much better than vegetarian wraps, no offense, sis."

"How would you girls like to visit the Nathan Hale Schoolhouse this afternoon? I can report to your dad we did something 'educational' as he suggested."

The twins nodded simultaneously, both thinking it would be a timely distraction.

"Oh, I almost forgot, there is a postcard on the table for you. I wonder who that could be from, looks like 'Old Ironsides' on the front."

Robin beat her sister to the dining area table and read the print out loud as Cresselley came up behind her.

"Coolest ship, lots of history here," it said. "You'd better be reading your way through the eighth-grade summer list! Home soon. Be good, Jesse."

"It's just as well he isn't here," Cresselley sighed. "He'd never approve of our history lesson with Charlie or our plans."

"Are you nervous, El? You really can stay behind, I mean it!"

"Drop it," Cresselley whispered.

Robbie and Elly
Find Out

It was another hot, humid day as the girls set off early the following afternoon. They'd given Carol a plausible explanation for why they'd be gone four hours. Counting out twenty paces up from the boat launch as Charlie had instructed, they easily identified the large boulder and the overgrown trail it marked.

"He wasn't kidding about the brambles, was he?" Robin observed. "I bet some of this damage is from the storm the other day. Looks pretty recent."

"Good thing he did warn us, otherwise we might have dressed for the heat, not slogging," Cresselley admitted.

The girls pushed on, struggling through the dense vegetation with a keen sense of purpose. They had a rough estimate of how far they had traveled by the steps recorded on Robin's Fitbit. In the lead, the older twin stopped abruptly.

"Here, El. The parallel stone walls Charlie mentioned. This must be the old North-South Road. We just turn right and follow it."

It was rough going, but the old thoroughfare was apparent referencing the parallel markers. Twice, Cresselley stopped to marvel at hefty, rusted horseshoes overlooked until she stepped on them.

"Robbie, look at the size of these things," she marveled.

"They probably belonged to big draft horses pulling weighty loads between the mills as Charlie explained. It must have been a sight to see. It's one-thirty, El, we should be getting close. Let's keep an eye and ear out. We don't want to be detected if someone is around."

With as much stealth as possible in the overgrowth, the girls continued, sensing they were getting close to their destination. The old roadway was becoming more apparent with deeper ruts and less debris. There were also subtle indications of numerous deer in the deep wooded area where narrow paths and stripped leaves marked their invisible presence. Abruptly, Cresselley stopped moving and a concerned look came over her face.

"What is it, El?" Robin whispered.

"Feels like it did that morning at the cave," the twin reflected.

On this occasion, Robin did not dismiss her sister's nervous demeaner.

"Over there," she pointed. "that big rock outcrop. We can scale it and have a vantage point of the area. If we're close, we should be able to spot the compound."

Cresselley nodded and the girls ascended the elevation. Lying on their stomachs at the edge of the ledge, Robin was first to look through the binoculars.

"It's visible," she reported. "Look, El, it's just as Charlie described. I can see the remains of the inn and even make out the old orchard," she added as she handed over the lenses.

"I see a woman at the side of the added-on living space," Cresselley whispered with excitement.

Robin wanted to respond, in fact she was trying to scream, but the heavy-booted foot pressing down between her shoulder blades prevented any audible sound. She felt a coarse rope tying her hands behind her back. Unable to turn and see what was happening to her twin, Robin struggled as hard as she could to fight off her assailant.

"Well, well, look who we have here," a voice remarked. "It's the little spying duo. Didn't get the message boss lady sent you in the restaurant?" It wasn't her captor speaking.

Robin reasoned by the direction of the voice. There must be two of them and the other had Cresselley.

"Where's your little boyfriend?" the voice came from directly above Robin, eliminating any doubt there were two of them.

Fighting desperately to turn her head and see what was happening to Cresselley, she was harshly yanked to her feet, only to discover her sister restrained in the same brutal manner. Before either girl could protest, a rag was stuffed in each of their mouths and tied at the back of their heads. Robin made eye contact with Cresselley. She looked frightened but thankfully, not freaking out. How had these barbarians snuck up on them? the young girl thought guiltily.

Dragged off the outcrop, the girls were brought directly to the compound. The back wing appearing exactly as Charlie had speculated; it looked lived in. As they approached, the door swung open and a woman wearing a Yankees cap appeared, she did not look pleased.

"Look what we caught," the rogue restraining Robin bragged. "Where you want them, boss?"

"You fools!" she growled angrily. "We don't have the time or resources to deal with this now. The second these two are overdue, the whole town and every law enforcement agency within a hundred miles will be out looking for them. Throw the little snoops in with the others, we need to move up our departure time, thanks to your stupidity. Are you sure they're alone?

"Yes, boss."

Out of the corner of her eye, Robin caught a glimpse of a third man rounding the side of the structure. Even from a distance, she was sure it was one the soccer players in their father's yearbook. Cresselley must have noticed as well, she caught Robin's gaze with a look of recognition.

"Oh good," the woman seemed pleased with his entrance. "Harold, I need you to hike out to the rendezvous point and see if the black SUV has been hidden off the road there yet. If it has, we need to leave just before dark."

The man nodded, turned on his heal, and departed.

Fearful of what "the others" might indicate, the twins didn't wait long to find out. They were abruptly dragged to an old-fashioned cellar door. The brute restraining Cresselley reached over, opened it, and pushed the young girl harshly down the short flight of stairs. Following close behind, Robin landed next to her sister with a thud. It was dark in the musty enclosure with just one small window for daylight. As their eyes adjusted to the dimness, the twins could unmistakably detect the figures of three young girls, crouching on a filthy mattress four feet in front of them. Visibly traumatized, they scuffled to the far end of the bedding.

Cresselley motioned to Robin to sit on a dilapidated wooden chair in the corner. When her sister was seated, she turned her back to her and worked at the knot in the gag with her tied hands. Within minutes, Robin spit the cloth on the floor. Switching places, Cresselley soon had her voice back as well.

"I wonder if they speak English?" She nodded to the girls and said softly," I'm Elly."

Picking up on her sister's lead, Robin self-identified adding, "We're American."

The oldest, judging by size, pointed to herself, "Eve, Laos," then indicating her closest companion, "Bopha," and the one huddled behind her, "Ab, they be Hmong, Cambodia," adding, "No English," to the introduction of her fellow captives.

"How long have you been here?" Robin asked turning around to indicate her Fitbit timepiece for visual clarification. Eve held up four fingers.

"I think she means four days," Cresselley inferred. "These poor girls."

"Elly, we need to find a way out of here before the move they plan or it won't go well for any of us. Judging by the conversation with that Harold dude, I'd say they plan to hike out to the SUV via the old west road. It must come out on Cassidy Hill, probably where Brit and Rachael spotted it. What worries me in that case is their plan for the two of us, we're a big liability now. If they leave us behind, they'll take the girls and be long gone by the time we can break free, if we even can, and notify the authorities."

"I agree, Robbie, we need to escape, all of us. Don't you think it likely this area is somehow connected to the dirt basement of the main inn? Even though it was built later, they must have needed access to rotate stored food and supplies. Maybe a door or a tunnel?"

"Makes sense, let's see if Eve can untie our hands."

It took some work, but once Elly's hands were free, she helped work on the stubborn knots restraining her sister.

"Stay with the girls, I'll explore the far wall. It's too dark to see any detail from here."

When Robin departed, Cresselley turned her attention back to Eve. "We're here to help," she explained with compassion. "We live close, by the lake."

"Seen the water," Eve reported with excitement. "Came by."

"Family?" Cresselley asked. "Robin is my sister." The twin wasn't sure how much Eve understood, but the young girl began to weep.

"Laos, Momma."

Before the conversation could continue, Robin reappeared dusty and sweating.

"There is a passage in the back wall," she reported. "And it does lead to the dirt basement under what's left of the main inn. I saw the kegs Charlie mentioned. We can get through there, but the stairs up to the first floor and outside look dubious. I don't see an alternative. We need to escape without notice."

"Did you spot any activity or sign that Harold dude has returned with news of the rendezvous?"

"Nothing, it's pretty quiet outside. I swore I could hear them talking in the living space, but it was muffled. Elly, we've got to convince these girls to attempt a break with us. It's clear we didn't stumble on a drug ring. This is human trafficking. If they don't escape before the final leg of their journey, it's unlikely they'll ever get away or see home again."

It took the twins precious time, even with Eve's assistance, to convince the terrified children of the immediate danger they were in if they remained captives in the basement. Finally, with Robin in the lead and Elly bringing up the rear, all five entered the narrow tunnel Robbie had discovered; it was dark and wet. Elly thought of the flashlight in her confiscated backpack recalling their father's insistence on having it along. What she wouldn't give to have him and it here now.

Thankfully, the passage was short. The still bright late afternoon sun was painful to the three sets of eyes, four days in the semi-darkness. The girls blinked and grimaced as they adjusted to the outside. Robin put her finger to her lips and pointed to the far side of the dirt basement. She was right, the stairs to the first level were in a state of decay, but there was no other way up. She signaled the others to follow her past the large disintegrating kegs, various glass mason jars, and what might have been storage shelves for produce. Robin cautiously tested each step as she had done on the fire tower a few days earlier. She made it to the top without incident and extended her hand toward Bopha. The vulnerable child hesitated briefly, glanced back at Ab then one by one, bravely mounted the stairs to Robin. The others followed in the same manner until all five were safely at the top. Cresselley indicated an overgrown cluster of bushes; Robin nodded her endorsement. The little party crouched and spoke softly planning their next move; there was no detectable activity from the house. The twins were confident they could retrace the route which had brought them to the compound despite being forcibly dragged the final leg. If they could get back to the parallel stone walls, the rest would be easy.

Robin glanced at her Fitbit; it would begin getting dark soon, there was no time to waste. Single file, she led the vigilant assembly past the massive, standing barn, through the edges of the once fruit-ful apple orchard, in the direction of the parallel stone walls. In the lead, Robin was first to spot three figures blocking their only means of escape. She and Cresselley might outrun them, but the others exhausted by their lengthy ordeal would never manage. Robin froze, motionless. Initially perplexed, the line behind her arrested as well. Bringing up the rear, Cresselley came forward and quickly grasped the delay.

"Tie 'em up," ordered Harold, taking charge. "Don't let them give us the slip again. I'll alert Boss Lady and we'll head out before any more setbacks."

The girls fought against the coarse ropes, but once again, they were no match for their assailants.

"See if you can get out of these, you little vermin," the taller of the two remaining abductors mocked.

No sooner had the words left his mouth, but a familiar voice ordered, "Put your hands where I can see them and back away." Officer Mendez materialized unexpectedly from the dense over-growth; he was holding a Taser.

Speechless and elated at his sudden appearance, the girls were suddenly overwhelmed. Though keenly aware it was a semi-auto-matic rifle in the hands of a domestic terrorist, responsible for the death of their mother and fourteen other innocent victims at a Black Lives Matter rally in New York City, the reality of the danger they had been in that chilling afternoon abruptly became apparent to the twins.

Before they could fully absorb these latest developments, an additional voice came from just behind them, "I would thank you to get your hands off my daughters!"

"Dad?" the twins were incredulous. "How in the name of prosecution?"

"Long story, girls," their father admitted while tightly squeezing his astonished, relieved daughters.

"Officer Mendez, there are two more in the wing at the back of the inn," Cresselley warned.

"We know, girls. Guess who is apprehending them as we speak?"

"Who?"

"Your FBI agent and a member of his field team"—Officer Mendez chuckled—"That was very clever how you ladies managed to contact him."

"Dad, what will happen to the little girls?" Cresselley whispered.

"We'll sort it out as soon as Agent Bruce joins us with an update. Don't worry, honey," he added gently, reluctant to release either of his daughters. "They'll be well taken care of. Lord only knows what they've endured. What's important is you are all safe now."

"So these are my clever, little assistant detectives," a generous voice acknowledged.

The twins turned to see a tall, middle-aged man approaching. "You girls managed to solve the last piece of this horrifying puzzle which eluded a large agency of the Federal Government! The two of you might consider a career in the criminal justice system—that is, after you finish college."

"My daughters are concerned about what comes next for…" Robert glanced in the direction of Eve, Ab, and Bopha.

"They'll be processed through a translator then individually assigned a female agent to escort them all the way home to their families in Southeast Asia."

"Where will they be 'processed'?" Cresselley asked.

"Most likely, New Haven. I'll go with them personally tonight. Agent Washington, who is holding the perpetrators at the back of the house, will transport the traffickers for arraignment with generous backup from Officer Mendez's unit."

"Can't you wait until morning?" Robin pleaded. "They could stay with us tonight—take a shower, have a decent meal, clean clothes, and a real bed."

"Please," Cresselley beseeched.

Agent Bruce's face softened. "I don't think a fifteen-hour respite will break any rules, the actual processing wouldn't begin tonight anyway. What do you think, Dad? Officer Mendez?"

"No objections here. Robert is an official of the court," Officer Mendez noted.

"I don't think you want to challenge my daughters' moral high ground in this particular context." Robert laughed. "They can be very sanctimonious when it comes to injustices."

"Very well then, ladies, I admire your compassion. I'll join my colleague and expedite the arraignment. These crimes just sicken me. Officer Mendez can sign the girls over to your dad temporarily once you're safely at the lake. I'll need to return tomorrow afternoon to take a formal statement and I'd like to meet the third member of your team."

"Jesse," the twins chimed together.

"Safe journey home," the agent added as he turned back toward the inn, "and thank you all sincerely."

Robert glanced at little Bopha, she was clearly terrified, confused, and exhausted. He knelt in front of her and offered a ride on his back. She hesitated briefly then smiled and accepted the offer. She bumped along; sound asleep on his shoulder for the remainder of the return trek to the boat launch, much to the twin's delight.

Robert and Officer Mendez assisted the girls on board "Blue Girl" for the final leg of the journey to the cottage. Fifteen minutes later, Carol eagerly met them at the dock. Agent Bruce had thoughtfully sent a field officer to update her, including an estimated time of arrival for the now party of seven. While the two men completed business, she escorted the five girls into the cottage. Laid out in three neat piles were clean nightclothes.

"The sizes might not be exact," she confessed, "but your grandmother will come by early in the morning with some of your outgrown outfits and essential toiletries for the girls' trip home."

Eve nodded graciously.

"But, Carol, how did you know?" Cresselley and Robin were astonished.

"You can thank your considerate FBI agent. Let's get these poor darlings cleaned up and fed. I made soup, sandwiches, and sliced strawberries."

After dinner, the twins escorted their reassured new friends to Cresselley's big bed. Eve guaranteed they would be perfectly content sleeping in the clean, comfortable bed together, particularly considering their accommodations for the last several weeks.

"We'll be right across the hall," Cresselley whispered.

Since their liberation, Eve had not taken her eyes off the twins for an instant. She nodded and tucked the three of them in.

"Elly," Robin whispered. "Let's tiptoe downstairs. I hear Dad and Carol talking. We need some details about how our rescue party found us."

"I'd like to know why Dad came home early for the Fourth of July picnic. He's rarely even on time!"

Their father was sitting in the middle of the couch when the twins entered the room. He put a loving arm around each of his daughters as they nestled in on either side. The room was quiet until Cresselley broke the silence.

"Dad, you came home early for the fourth."

"Truthfully, I'm two days late," Robert admitted. "Your sister asked me to come home for the weekend. I'm sorry, girls. Had I known…"

"Even if being here was a coincidence, how did you know where to find us?"

"Carol is your real hero. She recalled decoding your puzzle."

"I didn't have a clue about the XRD symbol, remember, girls?" Carol added. "Your dad knew right away."

"But how did the two of you know where to find the crumbling compound?" Their Dad was justifiably mystified.

Carol sat forward and slapped her knee. "Charlie Smyth," she exclaimed.

"You cunning little detectives. It was more than a friendly jam delivery. You girls knew you could get a history lesson from that generous man."

The twins initial silence confirmed a guilty verdict. Robin was first to continue.

"But, Dad, how was Agent Bruce informed?

"He wasn't, he pulled into the driveway ten minutes after I arrived from the train. He finally got your correspondence and tried to call your cell. As you know, it was in your room with a dead battery, so he couldn't track it. Guess where he stopped to ask for an address?"

"The post office," the girls gasped. "Grammy! She must be beside herself."

"Oddly, she didn't seem that surprised." Robert grinned. "Can't imagine why."

"Dad, please don't be mad at us. We know we stretched everyone's trust," Cresselley pleaded.

"How can I be angry with you?" Robert confessed. "What you and Jesse did for those three little girls and the dozens who would have followed is truly remarkable. I would agree with Agent Bruce, however, a college degree first would be advisable."

"No worries, Dad," Cresselley beamed. "I'm going to law school. Fieldwork isn't exactly my thing."

"And you, daughter number one?"

Robin squirmed next to her father. "I don't know about a career, but it was pretty awesome!"

"You lovelies must be exhausted," Carol hinted. "Your gram will be here early in the morning. She's bringing ingredients to make everyone a big breakfast."

Taking the implied recommendation, the twins hugged Carol and kissed their dad good night. Once in bed, they realized Carol was right.

Full Circle

The aroma of baking croissants lured Robin early from her bed. She was surprised to find not only her grandmother but Carol as well, busy in the kitchen.

"Good morning, sweetie," Grandmother chimed pleasantly. "Come here and give your grateful gram a big squeeze! Are the other girls awake? The clothes I put together are on the dining table. I hope they fit, I'm anxious to meet them."

"Thanks, Gram, that was so nice of you! I'll take them up. Carol, aren't you awesome in the kitchen this morning," the twin couldn't resist adding.

Carol shot Robin a look but laughed right along.

Fifteen minutes later, all five girls, dressed and rested, descended the stairs. The two youngest shyly greeted Grandmother, who gently kissed each one on the forehead. Eve twirled in her new outfit much to everyone's pleasure.

"Where's Dad this morning?" Cresselley asked.

"Check the dock, girls, he might be tying up. He and Blue Girl retrieved your kayaks." Carol smiled.

Robert was already busy with place settings when the girls passed into the dining area. He pulled out chairs and invited the three young guests to take a seat.

"Agent Bruce texted me earlier," he announced. "Three female agents will be here in about an hour to escort the girls through formalities and on their flight home. He wants us at Officer Mendez's town hall unit at one o'clock. He already contacted Jesse's dad. They returned from Quincy late last night."

"We'll be so glad to see Jesse," Cresselley admitted. "Seems like weeks, not days."

*****

It was difficult for the girls to say goodbye, but the female agents assured everyone home was only a few days away. Jesse and his parents were already in the town hall office when Robert and the girls arrived. There was more than enough evidence to convict the traffickers and put them in prison for a very long time. Agent Bruce simply required a statement and the opportunity to thank all three in person for their persistence.

"Do you budding detectives have any questions of me?"

"Just one," Jesse admitted. "The Barkers' house, the bear cave, boat launch, Crossroads—why all of these stepping-stones?"

"That's an excellent question, young man," Agent Bruce complimented. "It's not uncommon for traffickers to use what we call *waypoints* with their victims to avoid suspicion. They may lay low for a few days in each before completing the last leg of their pipeline, which is exactly what they were attempting to do with the hidden SUV when Robin and Cresselley intercepted them.

On the town hall steps, Jesse whispered to the twins, "We'll catch up later, you did not spend your time in the library."

Cresselley and Robin looked uncomfortable until Jesse grinned and gave a thumbs-up. "And guess what," Jesse added. "I talked to my dad, no more tech school. I can go here in town in September." The twins were overjoyed.

That afternoon, the girls were busy cleaning their kayaks when their father approached. "I've invited the Bosticks for our Fourth of July cookout and the lake fireworks tomorrow."

"Thank you, Dad!" The twins were ecstatic.

"Oh, and there is a little something for you in the trunk of my car," Robert added offhandedly as he turned over the keys.

Dashing to the driveway, the girls opened the back and looked inside. Lying flat on the spare tire was a large sign with hooks, which read:

Robert Spenser, Attorney-at-Law
2 Main Street, North Milltown, Connecticut

The twins looked at each other in disbelief. Their father was coming home.

The end

About the Author

Nancy E. Crofts grew up on a farm in a small Connecticut town. One of nine children, she spent her childhood doing chores, building tree houses, and reading mystery novels. The loss of her mother at the age of seven drew her into a close relationship with her grandmother Alice Larkham Crofts.

She has been an adjunct professor at the University of Connecticut and Three Rivers Community College for almost three decades, teaching social sciences.

Nancy is a licensed pilot, former Peace Corps volunteer, wife, mother, and foster care provider.

CPSIA information can be obtained
at www.ICGtesting.com
Printed in the USA
BVHW080047061121
620873BV00001B/35